The Weight of a Broken Heart

By Natacha Jean

Contents

CHAPTER ONE

JULIA

I put on my black sequin gown that goes past my knees. It's feels a bit uncomfortable on my skin, but I know that the shine of the black will bring out my skin color and make my eyes pop.

"How do I look?" I ask my friend, Maya, who is also getting ready to hit the club. Going out tonight was actually her idea. She's been pestering me about going out for quite a while now, so tonight I finally gave in.

"You look fabulous and wonderful, she gushes."

I smile at my friend. She's far more of a fashionista than I am or ever will be.

"Thank you. It is really itchy, but I think I'll be okay. As long as it looks good," I say.

Maya frowns then as she walks toward me in her beautiful red dress that will certainly steal the show in the club tonight. Her brows are furrowed, and I know that there is certainly something on her mind.

"What's the problem?" I ask. She'd convinced me to go to the club earlier that day, literally barging into the coffee shop and demanding that we go out. I was angry for a brief five seconds because that was why I like Maya— she's lively and bubbly and everything that I'm not. I need a friend to bring me out of my shell, and she's the one for me. I had decided that I'd go along, even though the club isn't my scene; the loud music, the lights, the alcohol, and the people, especially the people, are all too much for me. But in my three years as a college student, I had never been to one, and I actually want to do something spontaneous at the very least before I graduate. So, I'd said yes. And now I'm beginning to regret my decision.

"Uhmm, the dress. I don't know how to put it. It's nice and pretty and all, but it's a little plain." Maya clearly had something to say about my choice of attire, but she doesn't want me to feel bad, which is why she's hesitating.

"Maya," I say, adding a sigh as I roll my eyes.

She shrugs. "The dress is too shiny. I don't think you should wear it. I should have something in my closet," she rushes. And if I hadn't been listening carefully, I wouldn't have heard a thing she said.

I sigh again at her suggestion. That won't work at all. For lack of better words… Maya is voluptuous… and I'm… slim, thin, straight as a stick compared to her. That may or may not be the reason why I've been single for the last twenty-one years of my life. Or maybe it's because my head is buried in a book every day. The difference in our sizes means that I can't wear anything Maya owns. A dress might fit her to the skin but hang terribly on my body. There's no way she has a dress I can wear. It isn't even possible.

"You know that I can't wear your clothes, Maya. It won't fit well," I argue, plopping onto the bench in front of her mirror. I'm upset by how the night is going already, and I simply want to go home and rest. This is now feeling like a bother. The sequin dress had been a birthday gift to myself for my twenty-first birthday. I saved up to get it because, in between my normal bills and simply living, things are tight for me. They've always been like that, from when my parents died and I had to live with my grandma to when my grandma died when I was a freshman.

"Don't be upset, Julia. The dress is beautiful. I know how you bought it for yourself, but it's more of a dress for a gala or a dinner, not for a night out in a club," Maya says, and I nod. I feel better with her soothing words. That means the dress isn't so bad after all; I can wear it to dinner. If I'm ever invited to dinner.

"And about the fit, I have a little black dress that's just about your size," Maya explains as she digs around in her closet, and I look up at her in surprise. I knew that something was up, this is clearly suspicious.

"You have a dress in my size?" I ask, and she nods, looking all innocent as she smiles over her shoulder.

"Why do you have a dress in my size?" I ask again, and she shrugs.

"Oh, well, I just do," Maya tosses out as though I'm the odd one for asking. I suspect that there's more to it, but I nod and don't push it.

Maya sashays in her red dress to the other end of her closet and lets out a chirpy " Aha!" as she turns around with the much-discussed dress. I'm looking at it from afar, and I know that it is beautiful. And expensive.

"This is it," Maya says, helping me stand up. I take it from her and feel the soft material. It won't itch like the sequins, and I'll love how it'll feel against my skin. I'm sold and go into the bathroom to quickly change.

As Maya said, it fits my frame perfectly. I feel incredibly sexy in it, a new sensation for me, and I study how it hangs on me just right as I twist and turn in the mirror—the short skirt, the spaghetti-straps, and the little design in the front are perfect.

"Voila! You look magnificent!" Maya claps as I enter the room, and I can't help the blush that stains my cheeks. I walk to the full-length mirror, and I can say that I love the vision that I see. My blond hair is in waves over my back, my blue eyes stand out, and my body makes me look like a model—at the very least. I could pass for one. I don't look as sexy as Maya, but I look as perfect as I can get.

"This is good, this is so good. Let's pick shoes and bags, and we'll leave," Maya says with a grin on her face. She seems so excited to party, and for the first time, I share the same excitement with her. My excitement comes with nervousness, though; I've never been to a club before, and it feels like I might mess up if I do anything wrong , And I have cold feet for second as Maya touches up her makeup.

Should stay at home…? No. I push down the nerves and manage to make it to the club, I deserve some fun. And I need to break out of my comfort zone.

"We are here, baby!" Maya screams as we step out of the car that parked in front of the club, Essence. The club is a popular one, at least from what Maya told me; she's been here a couple times and claims the reception was wonderful. She always kept coming back.

"Let me tell you the truth, girl," Maya said back at the house. "It's the owner. I have a terrible crush on him; that's why I keep going back," she confessed, and I laughed. It was such a Maya thing to do.

"I can't wait to meet Calvin," I say to my friend as we go in. Maya frowns at me, but only for a minute, as the smile is back on her face almost immediately.

"Oh, he is so handsome! "she gushes, and I laugh again.

"You've said so; back at the house, I understand that he's handsome," I say, and Maya shakes her head.

"No, you don't get it." You'll understand when you see him. "He looks magnificent," Maya practically swoons.

Walking into the club feels like I'm entering another planet. The shift in the air is so obvious. I'm not sure if it's the colored lights or the fact that a whole lot of attention is on both of us, or maybe it's because the situation is so foreign to me. I like the feeling, though; it feels beautifully different.

"Let's go get ourselves a drink," Maya says. She's clearly oblivious to what I'm feeling and walks me to the bar. I try not to look around too much, but I can't help it; everything is shiny and loud, and it's all grabbing my attention at once.

"Okay," I say to Maya. This is another issue that I have with drinking. I can't handle my alcohol; it's as simple as that. I can get drunk with just a shot.

Maya orders something for both of us, and I'm grateful that she orders a drink with a low alcohol content.

"I can't have you throwing up on me when we go home, so please take little sips," Maya says as she hands me my drink, and I nod. I don't want to throw up either.

"Okay," I say, and start nursing my drink. Maya's eyes are busy on the dance floor. I can tell that she's looking for the owner of the club. I know exactly when she sees him, because her eyes light up. I smile at that; she really likes him.

"We should dance," Maya says then. That's her excuse to get on the dance floor so she can be with Calvin; it's a good excuse.

I want to say no because I can't dance to save my life, but Maya is my friend, and I can tell she really likes this guy, so I stand up with her. I'm willing to disgrace myself in front of the crowd for her; it's time to party.

The little alcohol in my drink also helps my decision; it loosens my inhibitions, and I don't care if I can't dance; I just want to move.

"Let's do this!" I shout a little too loud. Maya looks at me a little oddly, but I smile, and she nods.

"Let's go dancing!" Maya shouts a bit now, and we walk to the dance floor. The song is upbeat, and we begin to move our bodies to the music as I can see that she is moving toward a certain somebody. I don't know how, but I know Calvin the moment I set my eyes on him. There is a kind of power one exudes when one knows they're in charge. The aura is all around him, and he's incredibly handsome. Maya was right. In my opinion, though, the handsome man standing by his side is much better looking. He looks like he just stepped off a magazine cover, but a little out of place in the club in his navy blue suit. I can tell that there was a tie on his neck and he'd gotten rid of it. His hair is messy; I assume he got to the club immediately after work, and that managed to make him even sexier.

"Bye, love," Maya says, and I'm brought back to the present. I didn't realize that I was staring until Maya talked to me.

I stabilize myself and walk back to my seat. Seeing the man made me lose my appetite for dancing. I'm feeling a little lightheaded and sit down on the stool and order myself a martini. The handsome bartender pours my drink, and I begin to sip slowly. I find myself comparing the long blonde hair of the bartender to the short, wavy black hair of the man standing so close to Calvin. I turn back to get a glimpse of him, and I almost choke on my drink.

The man who can compete for the title of the most handsome man on the planet is right in front of me, walking toward me.

"Hi, I'm Alexander, but please call me Alex," he says, stretching his hand out for a shake. I feel very numb and just stare at his hand for a moment. I'm not sure what it is that I'm supposed to do.

"My name is Julia," I stutter when I manage to find myself. I can feel my heart beating rapidly and loudly against my ribcage. Why is he here? Why is he introducing himself to me?

Not even minding my low alcohol resistance, I down my drink in one go. I need all the courage I can get if I'm going to talk to this hot specimen of a man.

"How are you, Julia?" he asks, and the simple question seems like a whole lot more when he asks it. I feel my cheeks heat up. The way my name rolls off his tongue is something that should be studied. I can testify that I would pay to hear him say my name every day and twice on Sunday.

"I'm fine, I'm good," I say, and it's a wonder that the words that came out of my mouth were English. I want to order another drink because the alcohol in my system isn't nearly enough for this.

"You're very beautiful, Julia," Alex says, and this time I release an audible sigh; I can't help it. His voice is perfect—too perfect. I like to think that it's the atmosphere or the drink that pushes me to say my next words, but they're already out before I can take them back.

"You are very handsome, Alex." I cover my mouth immediately after the words are out, as though I'm trying to stop the words from traveling past the seams of my lips.

I feel like I could die of embarrassment. If I could bury myself under the table, I would, but I swallow my instinct to bolt and force a smile.

I look at Maya, and she is dancing with Calvin. They look so happy and free with each other. I know she won't be coming to rescue me anytime soon.

"I'm sorry; I didn't mean for it to come out like that," I apologize, and he shakes his head.

"It isn't a problem at all; you didn't do anything wrong; you flatter me. A lot of people say I'm handsome, but you caught me off guard, I guess. A beautiful woman is calling me handsome," he says, and I blush. He's very good with his words, I give him that. My eyes go to his lips; they're pink and inviting, and I imagine what it will be like to taste his lips at that moment.

He's looking at me too, and it's clear that he wants me to know it. His eyes are filled with lust, and I can't help but like the way he looks at me like I'm cream and he wants to lick me up. The thought of it makes me feel all hot and bothered. I want him; I'm sure of it. A reckless thought crosses my mind at that moment: I want him to be with me.

Since I was in a nightclub for the very first time, I may as well go all out and have my very first one-night stand.

Alex shifts his seat closer to mine, and his finger grazes the top of my thigh. He's looking straight at me. I can see the lust in his eyes; it's almost like the feeling is contagious, as I'm sure my eyes mirror the same.

There are no words shared between us, but he moves even closer and places his hand on my shoulder. Our faces are close to each other at this point; all it takes is a little bending, and a kiss will result.

"Kiss me," he says, and it's almost like an unknown force is moving me; I close my eyes and move closer to him. The last kiss I'd had was back in high school; it was my first and only kiss. I found out later that some boys had placed a bet on who would kiss me first, and I had fallen for the trap. I became more guarded after that experience, but this is different. This is something new.

Kissing Alex feels explosive. It's like fireworks are going off in my head and everything is just right because we are together; nothing can beat this feeling. His lips slant over mine, and he brings his hand up to cup my face. The feeling of his skin on mine is phenomenal. I can barely focus on the kiss; I want to feel everything at once. It doesn't occur to me that I'm kissing a total stranger; all I want is to feel his skin.

"Let me take you home, baby," Alex whispers in my ear after breaking the kiss. I want to pant at the lack of contact, but the words he whispers keep me wanting. I can't even complain. Alex could say that I should sell my soul to the devil, and at that moment I'd say yes. I'd do anything and everything that he wanted me to. and I'll definitely go home with him.

"Yes," I say, and he nods.

I look around for Maya, but I don't see her. I sent her a text saying that I'm leaving the club. I haven't fully recovered from the kiss, and the idea of doing something that is slightly taboo hasn't quite sunk in yet, so I don't even bother to second-guess what I'm about to do.

"Let's go home, baby."

CHAPTER TWO

I wake up with a throbbing headache. The pain is low, continuous, and incredibly annoying. My frustration builds as I struggle to open my eyes due to the rays of the sun stinging them. The smell of alcohol around me brings me to my senses.

I sit up almost immediately and force my eyes open. I look around, and I'm alone. The décor isn't familiar, but I know how I got here and who I got here with. What I don't know is why he left.

I try to stand up from the bed, and it only occurs to me then that I am naked. I hold the blanket to my bare breasts, and the sensations come alive then—my sore nipples and my equally sore core. They all remind me of what happened last night, of what I long to happen again and again. I'm even ashamed to be having these thoughts again, just after I'd done that.

"What did I do?" I groan, covering my head with my hands. The gravity of what happened last night is hitting me now—the fact that I, Julia Anderson, who had only one kiss in her life, lost my virginity on a one night stand with a man that I met only once. Alex, was it? I don't even know his surname. He probably thought I was a prostitute or something who was to be paid for those kinds of things.

"Oh, Lord!" I groan again. The more I think of it, the worse it becomes in my head. I don't even know why I did it. It was the alcohol and the adrenaline. But then again, I know very well why I did it; it wasn't the alcohol or the enthusiasm. I did it because I wanted to. I did it because he was hot, and I felt it wouldn't be so bad if I lived recklessly for a while.

I hold the blanket to my chest and waddle to the bathroom. It feels too intimate to walk naked in a room I have no clear memory of. This is hypocritical, as I am aware, because most of last night I was naked in this very room. I drop the blanket at the foot of the bathroom and step in. The mirror is the first thing I see. I let out a loud shriek as I study my reflection in the mirror. I look positively crazy, and fucked, too. My blond hair is like a huge nest; this is expected as Alexander spent so much time threading his fingers through it. My eyes are dilated, and I look like the cat that got the cream. Apart from the anger that I'm feeling, I'm pretty much satisfied and calm; the activity of last night has left me sated.

I raise my hand and then touch one of the red marks littered across my neck, shoulders, and breasts. Hickeys. From what I can remember, Alex loved making them; he loved kissing me and then seeing the marks they would form. I close my eyes as a memory of last night resurfaces. He was running his soft touch all over my body; his mouth leaving warm kisses over my neck, my chest, and my breasts, but not on my nipples, not where I wanted the pressure.

"You are so beautiful, Julia," he said then. I loved the way he complimented me and the way he called my name. I couldn't help but move closer and closer to him.

"Please love me, Alex." I pleaded; even if I was incredibly nervous, I had a feeling that he would turn me down, but I still asked. I wanted him so badly that I was willing to humiliate myself.

"All in good time, Julia."

I groan at the memory; I should simply stop thinking about it, and about him. It's already over. So what we had was a one-night stand. I should get over it.

I stomp my feet with anger and get into the shower. As I am taking a shower, it occurs to me that I am angry not because I just lost my virginity to a stranger; it was actually quite worth it for me, but because I want more than a one-night stand from him. I want to have a full-blown relationship with him, but he's gone. Maybe if he had stayed, we would have talked, and maybe he would have wanted more to do with me.

No, I shake my head; that isn't even possible. A man like that wouldn't want anything to do with me other than one night. I have to deal with that. I can't live in a fantasy.

I take my shower, dry off, and put on the little black dress that Maya had given me. *Maya.* I left her at the club last night.

I rush and pull my phone from my purse. I need to know if she's okay.

I open my phone, and the text that I see has me relaxing.

Okay, girl, have fun. I'm going to the house.

So, Maya is fine, and she knows that I'm fine.

I wear my dress and my heels and find a way to reduce my mass of hair since there's no hairbrush in the hotel room. I'm ready, and I take a deep breath as I walk out of the room. I'm scared to leave the hotel, as the walk of shame isn't something that I ever felt I would do. But here I am, walking out of a hotel room wearing the same clothes that I wore yesterday.

I feel the stares of people around me, but I have a feeling I'm imagining it; people do walks of shame all the time here; it is a hotel.

I resent Alex just a little, then. He should have taken me home like a gentleman, but instead, he ran away.

I exit the hotel in one piece and hail a cab to take me home.

Life after sex is an eye-opener; at least I can agree with that. After my first time with Alex a month ago, I've been missing him terribly. I see the man everywhere, and every time, the amount of horniness that I feel doesn't help my case. I can't control how much I want to have sex with him, of all people. But Alexander is unreachable, and he isn't the kind of man that I could even want.

"I want one cup of coffee, please, with cream and sugar," one of the customers at the coffee shop where I work part-time says, bringing me out of my little escape from reality.

I take her order down immediately and begin to work on it.

I remember what I saw on the internet after the first week, and I was going crazy with no information on him at all. It took a while before I told Maya about it. She was so excited for me, that I was coming out of my shell, that I was changing. She literally wanted to throw a party for me.

When I told her that I was thinking about him too much, she looked down on me, like I was doing something that was absolutely wrong and that it was bad for me to be obsessing. I can't help it, though. His brown eyes and sweet smile won't seem to leave my mind.

"That's not how it works, honey. It was just a one-night stand, and you can't be thinking of him anymore. He won't be thinking of you, either. You should move on, Julia." The bubbly and sweet Maya was calm, which was enough to show that she was serious. And I was devastated.

I have to let it go.

At least I tried. But before I'd confessed to her, I had wanted to know his last name. I wanted to know the man that I had sex with for the very first time.

It was easy to track him; he was Calvin's best friend, so all I needed to do was get information on Calvin. I found out that his name was Alexander Wright and that he was twenty-five years old, just three years older than me. I also found out that he had been friends with Calvin since they were children, and they were close. I discovered that he was the founder and owner of Wright Corporation. I found his pictures on his social media pages, and I was literally drooling because of how handsome he is. The tabloid stories on him showed that he was in a relationship a few years ago, as then he had pictures with just one particular woman, a model named Genevieve. It wasn't like I felt I could be with Alex, but after going through her pictures, I knew for a fact that a relationship between the both of us would not work at all. We are from two different worlds. Genevieve traveled the world, and I can't even stand in front of a runway. He is literally swimming in money, and I still can't afford necessities. He is too far away from me; I shouldn't even be thinking about him, not in this way.

So, we had mind-blowing sex with each other. It was something that I could only experience once in my lifetime. But then again, he could have simply waited till I woke up and not left me like a hooker in the hotel. Maybe I could have kissed him while sober and held him tight. But he just had to leave me like that. Even though I wasn't the kind of girl that he usually rolled with, he could have made an exception for me. At least to let me know he was leaving. No, he was definitely a jerk—a very handsome jerk, but nonetheless a jerk.

I finish preparing the cup of coffee and start to take it to the customer. Back to reality now; I can't keep on living in a fantasy. I walk out to the table where the customer is sitting, and I'm almost there when everything starts to get blurry. I don't even have time to catch myself when it all goes black.

"Julia, Julia." I hear my name, and I struggle to wake up from the strong spell of sleep.

"I want to sleep," I groan, and I snuggle more comfortably into my soft bed.

"I know that you aren't well, but this is urgent, Julia," Maya says, and I try to open my eyes. I'm really tired, as I have been for the past few days. I try to sit up on my bed, and bile rises up my throat. I stand quickly and rush to the bathroom. I'm bending over the sink almost immediately and puking what feels like my guts out.

Maya is in the bathroom with me and removes the hair that is falling down and rubs my back.

"Thank you," I say, as usual. I didn't actually vomit, but then again, I haven't had the appetite to eat, so there's nothing that I could have vomited.

I rinse my mouth and walk back to my bed.

I fainted at my place of work last week, but I woke up on my own and told my boss not to worry about it. They had already called Maya, and my friend appeared almost immediately to take me home. My boss gave me a break and asked me not to come back until I got better. I haven't been able to go to a class since I fainted, and I've been trying to recuperate. I really hate drugs and hospitals, so I've been at home. I know that I'll be fine soon, though. My body is pretty strong, and I barely get sick at all. Another thing that gives me hope is the fact that I'm gaining weight. I don't eat well, and I keep throwing up, yet I'm feeling bigger. The weight gain couldn't be a bad thing; it means I'll be fine soon.

I am walking out of the bathroom when Maya holds me back. I turn back and look at her in shock, her hand on my wrist.

"What is it?" I ask, because my friend has had this look on her face ever since I've been sick, it's like she knows something that I don't. Worst of all, she clearly doesn't like this knowledge that she had.

"Julia, there's something I want to tell you," Maya says. It's clear she has something important to say, but I don't want to have a conversation in the bathroom.

"Can we talk about it outside? I need to sit down," I say. My sense of smell has also been heightened. It's almost like smelling is my new superpower; some smells that I didn't know before have become heightened.

"You'll need the bathroom after the talk," Maya says, and I stare at her suspiciously. I don't even understand where she's coming from or what exactly she means.

"Then I'll come back inside the bathroom after the talk," I say, and Maya sighs.

"Okay."

We both walk out, and I sit down on the bed.

"What is it?" The tension of what Maya wants to say is killing me; the look on her face is so serious and so unlike her.

"What do you think is wrong with you?" Maya asks, and I breathe in. I don't understand her question, or the conversation in general.

"I have the flu; that much is obvious," I say offhandedly. It's not like anything else could be wrong with me.

"But you're vomiting," Maya says, and I shrug.

"Perhaps I have food poisoning as well." At this point, the conversation as a whole is making me feel increasingly aggravated. "But what does it matter? I'm sick, and that's the end of the story. I just need to get better." Like every sick person, I can't wait to get my health back again, so all the questions tend to annoy me.

"So, you don't think it could be something else?" Maya asks, and I narrow my eyes.

"Like what?" I am shouting at this point. But Maya isn't moving; she sits calmly and looks me in the eye.

"You know, like being pregnant," she says offhandedly.

Shock cannot even cover the emotions that I feel at that moment.

"No, of course not; I can't be pregnant," I say, and even as I say the words, I know that there is a possibility. *That night, and then all the symptoms…* I know little about pregnancy, but at least from movies, the nausea was sure, as were tiredness, an increased sense of smell, dizziness, and all the other things I've been feeling.

Maya doesn't even bother to say that I'm wrong, that I am pregnant. It's almost like she's waiting for me to figure it out on my own.

"I can't be pregnant," I say again, but this time the words are weak. I don't even believe them myself. *Maybe I am pregnant.* I suddenly feel like crying. What will I do if I am? I'm only twenty-one; I don't have any family left; I can barely take care of myself; and a baby is not what I need right now. God knows that, and he will make sure that I'm not pregnant.

"What do I do?" I ask Maya then. The questions are racing through my head, and I'm struggling to be calm.

"We need to be sure first before we can even think of anything, so I brought a test—well, two," Maya says, pulling out a little plastic bag from her purse. I collect it from her and see two pregnancy tests inside. I know that being pregnant means I will see two red lines, but I'm so scared as I take the test that my hands are shaking.

"I need to go to the bathroom," I say, and Maya nods. When I stand up this time, it's with shaky legs, and I walk to the bathroom and sit on the toilet seat. My pee seems to be afraid of the test. And I sit there for so long trying to get myself to pee, but nothing happens; I can't even force a drop out of my body.

"What's going on in there?" Maya asks after knocking on the door.

"I can't pee. I'm trying so hard, but nothing is coming out," I shout to her.

"Just come out then; you can try it again later." I don't want to do that at all; I'll die from the tension of not knowing if life is growing in me or not. I consider Maya's option, though. If I come out and drink loads of water, I can get this over with soon.

I stand up from the toilet seat, and I suddenly feel pressed. I release this time, and my bladder lets go. The two sticks are wet with urine now, and I put them on the counter and start the timer.

"I peed!" I shout to Maya to let her know the progress, but my heart is beating so fast inside my chest that it feels like it will explode and release. The next five minutes of my life feel like the longest five minutes I have ever experienced.

"Please don't let me be pregnant. One line, please, one line, please." I close my eyes and pray. The tension barely even lets me pray, as I open my eyes after the prayer. I glance at the pregnancy tests, but there are no lines yet. Five minutes are turning into five years, and that might even be better than what I'm facing. I close my eyes again, and this time when I open them, I see lines. In the first test, I see one line and shout. "Negative!"

Maya hears me, and she is shouting outside the bathroom, too, celebrating my lack of pregnancy with me. Yes, I am so happy. I'm just sick, and the dizziness, nausea, sensitivity to smell, and fainting were all parts of being sick; that's all that's wrong with me. I didn't even miss my period. It was a little late, and it wasn't very heavy, but it came.

"Positive?" I look at the second test. That doesn't make any sense at all. How can I be pregnant? Why does one test say something and the other test say the opposite?

"Positive?" Maya asks, and I open the bathroom door for her to enter and see. She looks at the two tests and nods.

"It can be like that sometimes. Let me get more tests to confirm," Maya says, and I groan out loud. I have to pee again.

"Buy different types, like ten this time." I need to be sure of the negative," I say, discarding the tests, washing my hands, and going out to the living room.

"Of course," Maya says.

"I can't be pregnant; I had my period," I argue as Maya is leaving, and she nods.

"We will just confirm," she says, and she closes the door on her way out.

I remind myself of the fact that I saw my period and used a pad for like two days, so it means that there was no baby formed. No life was growing inside me, and I don't need to worry about anything else. I'll be fine in the end.

Maya comes back later, and I've downed about six bottles of water in preparation for the urine I'm about to pass to the tests.

"Do you think you can do six?" Maya asks, and I nod.

"Bring it on," I say. This time, the process is a lot easier, as I actually know what I'm doing. I pee on the six sticks and set my timer. I come out of the bathroom, and both Maya and I walk in after the timer has rung. The range of test results that I see only added to my earlier confusion.

"Four positives, two negatives," Maya says, and I groan.

"Is something wrong with my pee?" I'm frustrated.

"I'm pretty sure that your pee is fine, but if you are pregnant, you couldn't be more than a month gone; maybe that's it, and I read somewhere that the more diluted the urine is, the less accurate the test results." I don't even want to hear what Maya is saying; all I want to know is if I'm cleared of being pregnant.

"I am not pregnant; I saw my period," I repeat petulantly. I'm just putting it out there, and I'm also trying to reassure myself.

"We should go to the hospital to do a blood test instead; we can't be too careful," Maya says, and I shake my head. I don't want to go to the hospital. I'm scared of needles and drugs.

"Can't we go somewhere else? A place that isn't the hospital?" I ask, because I really don't want to see a doctor.

"We're going to the hospital first thing tomorrow morning; get ready, and I will not take no for an answer," Maya says, picking up her bag. She's not going to listen to any other argument that I have to make.

Oh well, it seems like I'm going to the hospital.

CHAPTER THREE

I sit down comfortably in the waiting room with Maya by my side. The smell of antiseptic and the sight of sick people around me make me nauseous. I try to control myself and be calm, though it's not easy at all. I close my eyes tightly as I remember the prick of the needle when my blood was being collected for the pregnancy test. I try to keep calm by reminding myself that I am not and can't be pregnant, but the words of the doctor keep repeating over and over again in my mind.

"Many women still see their periods in the first months of their pregnancy, but that isn't their period; it is light spotting that usually comes early in pregnancy but stops after."

"Oh," I said. I didn't have anything else I could to say then; I just have to accept that I may be pregnant.

"We will do a blood test to confirm," he said, and I nodded.

The blood test was the part that I dreaded the most, but I was able to endure it without screaming down the entire hospital, so that was good enough for me.

"Julia Anderson." When the receptionist calls out my name, I immediately stand up. My heart is beating just like it did when I was waiting for the home test, maybe a little bit more.

"Yes, ma'am," I answer.

"The doctor will see you now," she says, and I look to Maya, who nods at me. I walk to the doctor's office and sit down.

"How are you feeling now, Julia?" the doctor asks, and I struggle to smile.

"I'm fine, just a little nervous," I say. It's not the total truth; I'm more than a little nervous, I'm a whole lot nervous—more nervous than I've ever been.

"Okay, your test results are back," he says, and then he hands me the envelope. I take it from him with shaky hands and open it. I pull out the single sheet of paper and wish then that Maya had come in with me. It'd be easier to do this with her. I stare down at the piece of paper and blink. I'm pregnant. That is what the test says.

"You will have fixed days to come for your checkup and scans; you can bring your significant other with you or a friend if you want," the doctor says, and he sounds so happy for me. On a level that is too high to even comprehend, I'm suddenly happy to be pregnant and briefly wonder if my hormones are messing with me. Tears to joy in seconds. But prior to this craziness, I'd always had a baby fever. Growing up alone as an only child was something that I didn't enjoy, and it wasn't easy for me. When my parents were alive, I used to wish for younger siblings. After they died, I knew I would be alone forever. No brother, no sister. Just me. This was when I started to want a child. The baby would have come later when I was settled and could actually care for it, but I didn't see this coming, yet I'm still happy. I'm scared beyond a reasonable doubt, yet I'm happy. I know that I don't have any plans for the child, and there's no way I can raise a child all on my own, yet it still feels like a dream come true.

The fear overshadows the happiness, but the baby is here, and there's nothing I can do about it.

"Thank you, doctor," I say, and I stand up and leave the office. I walk out and see Maya looking at me. She looks scared, and I wonder what is going on in her mind. I smile at her, and she visibly seems calmer.

"What did the results say?" she asks, and I sigh.

"You're going to be an aunt," I tell her with a smile. I can't cry anymore, so smiling is the best thing to do.

"You seem too relaxed for someone who is about to become a single mother," Maya says. I can tell that she's struggling not to shout and that she's angry, but I don't get why. I'm frustrated myself, but there's nothing I can do about the situation. I can't fall apart, start crying, and feel sorry for myself. It is a shock, and it's scary, but I have to deal with the facts now that have answers.

"Let's go home," she says and picks up her bag from the chair. She starts walking out of the hospital, and I follow her until we get to her car. The drive back home is quiet and full of many unspoken words. A knife could cut through the tension.

"So, what do you want to do?" Maya asks me, and I shrug.

"What else? I'm going to have the baby," I say. It' obviously the only option that I have. While I won't condemn those who commit abortions, it isn't something that I will ever consider doing myself. I want the child. I didn't even know that there was a child in me until now, but I want the child. I want to carry my baby. I'm twenty-one years old, a consenting adult, free to have a child of my own, and I'm going to do just that.

"You're going to have a baby on your own?" Maya asks. I don't like that she's making the situation worse than it actually is.

"Yes, I am. What's so bad about having a baby?" I ask.

"I don't know, maybe the fact that you're still a student and you didn't even consider pregnancy before I told you about it," Maya argues.

I shrug. That doesn't change anything at all. "What would you have me do?" I ask, and she stares at me like I shouldn't expect her to say the words, like I should know what to do.

"An abortion, of course," she says out loud after a while.

"I don't want to get an abortion. I'm not going to get one," I say simply, and I leave the car. I don't want to keep talking about it over and over again. I won't have an abortion.

"I respect your decision, but you have to think this over; having a child is not as easy as you think it is. And you're still in college; you need to finish and get a job, maybe a stable partner, it'd be best to have a child then," Maya says, and I nod. I understand. She wants the best for me, even if it's not the same best that I want.

"I am an adult, Maya, I can have a child. I can raise the child even if I don't have anyone; the child can be the person that I have. And if I need help, I can always tell the father. I need to tell him as soon as possible that I am pregnant and that I am having the baby," I say, and Maya looks a bit scared. I know that the fear she is feeling is for me.

"I accept your decision, Julia, but I don't know about your baby's father; how will you meet him?" Do you think he'll believe you when you tell him that you are pregnant by him? The way one-night stands go is that you never talk to the person again and you both leave each other for life. Telling him that you're pregnant is violating that code," Maya says, and I nod. I don't totally understand the code of one-night stands, since I'd never had one before, but I know what she's talking about. Maybe Alex will be reasonable. I'm sure of it. When I tell him that he's going to be a father, he'll tell me that I can keep the child. He could even visit the baby every once in a while.

"It's not like I'm asking him for a happily ever after, that we should get married, or something odd like that. All that I want is to tell him that he will be a father, and maybe he'll want to be present in the life of his child," I say, and she nods. She looks skeptical, but she's still calm.

"You can go and talk to him, but don't expect anything at all from him, so you don't get hurt. The more you expect from humans, the more they hurt you. Let's just say he will agree to be the father of your child and that he will take responsibility. How do you plan to find him?" Maya asks. I hadn't really thought about it, but I can't just go knock on his door, even if his address was on social media. No one would let me in. I'd have to meet him in a public place, and the only public place that came to mind is Essence, the club where we met in the first place.

"You said you were still involved with Calvin?" I ask my friend, and she shakes her head.

"No, no, no, I'm not getting involved in this at all. I only just got Calvin's number," Maya complains.

"You'll be fine in the end. You have to do this for your goddaughter," I joke.

"How do you even know it is a girl?" Maya asks, incredulous.

"I just have a feeling," I say.

"I'm not doing it," Maya says.

"Oh, you are."

***

ALEXANDER

I'm having one of the longest days, as I spent the past five hours trying to tackle the issue of mismanagement of funds in my establishment. I hate it when things aren't in order, and if there is disorder, that is certainly what's happening in Wright's Corporation at this point. I've tried my best and at least got a little success from today's work.

I'm on my way home so I can have a long shower and all into bed. But then my phone rings. It is Calvin.

"Hey, Calvin. What's up?" I ask. Calvin and Kenley have been close friends since we were children. Even as adults, we still have a tight relationship with each other. I go to Calvin's Club often to unwind, and I've been going there more frequently than usual because of the pretty blonde I met a month ago. I'm unable to get her off my mind. Even after our night together, I still want to see her. The post-nut clarity didn't work this time.

Calvin's call is unusual, since I'm usually at the club; it must be urgent for him to call me.

"I'm good." You need to come to the club as soon as possible, Alex. "It's urgent," Calvin says, and I frown. I don't know the reason for his call, but if Calvin says it's urgent, I have to go.

"I'm on my way," I say, and then take an alternative route to Essence. My friend owns several clubs across town and even across the country, but he's particularly attached to Essence, as it was the first club he opened. After going to business school, his father expected him to take over the running of the company, but Calvin was interested in doing other things, so he started by opening the club. It wasn't easy without the blessing of his parents, but he was able to manage it. It's one of the reasons why I'm so proud of him. I throw my key to the valet as I stop in front of Essence. My pace increases as I walk inside the club. I need to hurry, as Calvin said it was urgent.

"Where's your boss?" I ask the bouncer as I'm about to enter.

"The boss is upstairs," he says, and I nod. I go into the club, and the music is blaring loudly, the colored lights giving the place a different vibe. I walk upstairs to Calvin's office and knock before I enter.

"What's so urgent?" I ask as I step inside. But then, no more words can come out of my mouth, as I see two ladies in Calvin's office. One particular face catches my eye. It's the beautiful Julia. She looks a bit different from when I last saw her in the club. She's wearing a sweatshirt and jeans now; her hair is packed up in a ponytail, and there isn't an atom of makeup on her face. She looks a lot younger than I thought that night. I can't see very well, with the lighting, but I can tell that she looks sick.

What is she doing here?

Is she the urgent matter that can't wait for me to go home first?

21

My mind is going to different places all at once, but there's one place where it rests, and that is the reason why I don't do one night stands. I only sleep with women whom I am sure share mutual interests. I don't want to be in a relationship, and I know that I'm not willing to give more than that.

"Thank God you're here, Alex. Julia is here; she wants to see you," Calvin says, and I glare at my friend. If I had known that she was the one who wanted to see me, I would have refused to come. I'm not in the mood to deal with a woman who most probably feels scorned.

"Alex, good evening," Julia says, and I look at her. Even without all the apparel from the day I met her, she still looks beautiful, almost perfect. And if not for the situation, I would ask her for another night. I would definitely break my rules for her, but just looking at her, I already know the answer. There's no way in hell that she will agree.

"Julia, it's been a while." To be precise, one month. I haven't been with another woman for a whole month because I missed the woman standing in front of me.

"Yes, it has been a while. A lot has happened," Julia says, and I nod. A lot has happened on my part too.

"We will give you guys some privacy," Calvin says, holding the hand of the other lady sitting next to Julia. She's glaring at me like she wants to bury me, and it's clear she's a friend of Julia and this is her not so subtle way of warning me not to hurt her friend. Oh well, that depends on what her friend wants to tell me, though I have a pretty good idea.

"Have a seat," I say to Julia after Calvin and the other lady leave.

Julia sits down slowly, and she begins to tap her hands on the table, as though she's nervous. I don't blame her; I would be too if I were in her shoes. If you're planning to pin a baby on a business mogul, your acting has to be top-notch. She hasn't said anything, but I know how this works. I've been through this many times, even with women that I didn't even have sex with. And I've managed to get through all of them; this won't be the first, and it probably won't be the last.

"So what is it that you want to tell me?" I ask. She's too quiet. It's almost like she wants to change her mind, like she doesn't want to tell me anymore. So I prod her so she can lie, I can debunk her lies, and then I can go

22

home and finally rest; it's been a long day.

"I have been sick. So I went to the hospital. The doctor said that I'm pregnant," she whispers, and if I didn't know what she wanted to say, I might not have heard her. She puts an envelope on the table, which is probably the pregnancy result. I pick it up and look at it. Positive. She is pregnant, at least by the result.

"The baby is not mine. I used a condom," I say immediately. I'm always careful with one-night stands. There is no understanding, like with couples, to be faithful to one another.

"That isn't possible; the baby is yours," she says. She's clearly shocked by my words. I think she didn't expect that I would say that I used a condom like it wasn't the normal way to have sex.

"I'm sure that I'm not the only one you had sex with during that time period. Why don't you go ask all your potential baby daddies? But it's not mine," I say, and I get up. She looks broken by my words; a drop of tears covers her eyes, and she looks like she's about to break down. I feel guilty about my choice of words; maybe I could have gone easier on her.

"You are the only one I have been with, ever." The words almost make me laugh out loud. The woman that I slept with was a virgin, but that doesn't mean she didn't have sex with someone else after that day. The guilt that I'm feeling for her disappears. She should have tried to be more thorough in her business of scamming people.

"Julia, listen. You should go and tell your lies to those who actually want to listen or are foolish enough to believe them. They'll never work on me," I say, turning from her as I begin to walk out of the office. I can hear her crying, but I decide to block my ears from that. The woman is good at acting and manipulating with tears. My experience with Genevieve, who is now my ex-girlfriend, taught me a lot, and from this point forward, I won't let another woman manipulate me.

I walk out of the office and see that Calvin and the other lady were listening at the door.

The lady is glaring at me with cold eyes, but I couldn't care less.

"Did you know what that woman wanted to tell me, Calvin?" I ask my friend as the lady goes into the office to meet her lying friend.

"I did; I figured you should hear it for yourself," Calvin says.

"You shouldn't have wasted your time. Next time, just don't call me; send them home. I have had a long day, and I need sleep," I say.

"So it's not yours?" Calvin asks, and I shake my head.

"That's not even possible. The baby isn't mine," I say, and my friend nods.

I walk out of the club to drive home. During the drive, I can't help but think of how pained she looked when she was crying and when I told her that the child wasn't mine. I feel the guilt that I had previously suppressed—what if she wasn't lying? What if the baby was mine?

CHAPTER FOUR

JULIA

I feel like the whole world is turning upside down. I'm drained, weak, tired, and I'm starting to regret my decision to keep my baby, even if it hasn't been long since I made the decision. I didn't really expect much from Alex, but I also didn't expect the man who treated me with so much care and who took my virginity to become the monster who spoke to me today. His words broke me in ways that I can't explain. I was so hurt. He made me feel like I was dirty and undeserving of him. He's so sure the baby isn't his. It is crazy how he can just assume that I was lying. The way he laughed when I said I had only been with him made me even angrier; that was the height for me. Tears fell down my cheeks, and I tried to remain calm. My willpower didn't help, though; the tears fell more and more, and I began to choke on them.

"Julia!" I can hear Maya screaming as she runs to me. I can't find the strength to raise my head as she approaches, then the hands of my friend wrap around my shoulders, and I lean into her. I need the contact; I really need a hug right now.

"What did that bastard say to her?" Maya shouts angrily. I know that she's speaking to Calvin, and I agree that Alex is a bastard. That is the now only way I will agree to describe him.

"Calm down," Calvin says. His voice is low, and I know that he's trying to advocate for peace.

"We should go," I say as I sniff. I clean my face with a tissue and stand up. Maya looks at me oddly, as though she can't believe what I'm saying.

"That bastard shouldn't treat you so badly and get away with it!" Maya says, and I agree with her. Alex shouldn't get away with it, but there's nothing I can do. I can't force him to accept my child, and Maya can't keep shouting at Calvin, who isn't even the father.

I know that it seems like he's right, that Alex is right and that he's not the father if I give up so easily, but I can't bring myself to care less. I just want to go home and cry my eyes out.

"Let's go home, Maya," I say again, and my friend looks at me with understanding in her eyes. She nods, and we leave together.

As I leave Essence, I have a feeling that it will be a turning point in my life and that many things will no longer be the same.

I'm starting a new life at this point—a life of being a mother and a life of living for more than myself. I have to brace myself for it.

I go home and cry on my bed. I don't know how long, but I cry so much that it feels like I couldn't cry again.

The days go by and feel like they don't exist. Maya is with me all the time, and she comforts me so that I don't break down. I do, though, and she's there to hold me. I feel myself go through the five stages of grief, like I lost a loved one rather than the father of my child leaving me. It happens to a lot of people; I just never imagined it happening to me. I wonder if I overreacted when it's all over, but then again, I know that the pregnancy also affected my emotions. They were all over the place; even when I managed to pull through my depressive phase, I was still crying at anything and everything. It didn't help that I was always sick. After his denial, all I did was sleep, throw up, and lie around all day. I had stomach cramps, I was always dizzy, and I was never actually okay. Too many things were happening to me at once, and it was so hard to deal with them.

I contemplated having an abortion then, but, surprisingly, Maya was the one who stopped me.

I felt at times that I should just let the baby go; it was quite obvious that his father didn't want it. I wasn't even sure if I could care for it. I told Maya one morning when I was in my second month that I was more stable than in the beginning, but I was still very hurt by what happened. The little liking that I had for Alex was already gone.

I was pretty sure that Maya would support me, and a little support was all I needed—a hand to hold as I went to the hospital.

No, Julia, you aren't fit enough to be making decisions. You wanted to keep the baby when you were okay, and you may regret this decision later. Don't let that bastard kill the love that you have for your child," Maya said then, and I cried. I couldn't help it; her words hit me hard, and tears began to flow from my eyes and down my cheeks. Maya held me almost immediately. As usual, she knew that I needed contact.

"Thank you," I said to my friend, and she smiled.

And that was how I decided to keep my baby.

"I am so excited," I say to Maya, who is a proud godmother-to-be. We are at the hospital's reception, waiting for my turn to see the doctor. Today is when I do my first ultrasound. I'm already nine weeks in, and it is a little late, but it has been really hard to get myself moving after what happened. I can't wait to hear the heartbeat of my child and see how they look. I'm so excited about this, as it will make it a whole lot more real. I have a little bump already, and it's so crazy that there's a child inside me. This test will just validate that for me.

"I can't wait either," Maya says. I'm so grateful for the gift of a friend; without Maya, I'm not sure I would've been able to go this far in the pregnancy. She was able to help me with finances, her time, and her presence. She's always there for me, never tired of taking care of me and my unborn child.

"Julia Anderson, you may go," the receptionist says, and I stand up with Maya and walk into the doctor's office. She's so nice and helpful as I change into the hospital gown and lie down on the bed. I can feel my heart rate rapidly increase as she puts the cold jelly on my stomach and then starts to move the wand.

A loud thumping sound fills the room, and I feel tears stain my eyes. Happy tears this time.

"That is the heartbeat of your baby," the doctor says. She looks confused, though, as she is still listening.

"It seems like you have more than one heartbeat," she explains, and I look at her in shock. I almost start laughing, but I can't bring myself to laugh. The situation is too serious. What does more than one heartbeat mean?

"Let's take a look at your scan," she says, and I nod, even though I'm shaking with fear inside. The black and white picture of my uterus comes up on the screen. I can't really make much out of it.

"Congratulations, Ms. Anderson; you are expecting triplets," the doctor says.

"What?" Maya and I shout together. I can barely believe my ears; in fact, I don't want to believe my ears at all. Triplets? I'm not expecting one child, but three? How did it go from one to three? But that's not possible.

"I can't be having triplets; I just had sex once," I say. I know that it doesn't make sense and that I can get pregnant with triplets by having intercourse just once, but nothing at all makes sense to me right now. I just want to wake up from this dream, because this cannot be true.

"That's not how it works, Ms. Anderson. Although giving birth to multiple babies at once is rare, it does happen, and it is something that most people don't expect. If you don't have the resources to take care of all of them, you can always put them up for adoption," she says, and I nod. I can't imagine separating my triplets. I'm already imagining giving birth to three children at once. I wonder if I will be able to do it. The birth process scares me now, and I feel fear lying on the bed. I sit upright almost immediately. I don't want to die during birth.

The physician appears to be reading my thoughts when she informs me that I would most likely give birth via cesarean section. I smile at her then and nod.

"Thank you," I say.

When I leave the doctor's office, I'm still dazed. Maya is shocked too, just like me—three children all at once. That's huge. I didn't prepare for this. I'd signed up for one child, but three?

How would I take care of them? I still have school to think of. What about the finances? Baby things are expensive, and I have to raise them until they're grown.

My mind goes to Alex then, and I frown. I hate that he left me alone, I want to tell him that I'm having triplets, but I know that I can't.

It would be reasonable if he would deny one child, but he would deny even harder against three. He doesn't deserve my babies; I already decided that a long time ago, and he already signed away his rights to them. He doesn't deserve to be their father.

Even if their father is absent, my children still deserve a good life. How can I give it to them alone? All these thoughts are going through my mind as we drive back to our apartment.

"You shouldn't give the babies up for adoption, even if they are three. I will help you out; we will take care of my godchildren together," Maya says to me, and I stare at her, shocked. It's obvious that she changed her mind about the pregnancy, but I didn't think that my friend would go this far. She loves my children like her own, and they aren't even here yet.

I look up at her and say, "Thank you," as I feel the tears welling up once more in my eyes. I explain, "It's the hormones," and hug Maya as tightly. I have to squeeze her as hard as I can right now. To the moon and back, that's how much I love my friend. "Thank you, Maya," I say again.

"It is okay, Julia," she says, holding me tight. I count my blessings, and I hold my friend a bit longer.

The next few months are tumultuous, to say the least, and I struggle for normalcy, which isn't easy. I find out that being pregnant in school is more difficult than I thought it would be; being pregnant with triplets and being in your penultimate year is the worst. The cravings, the tiredness, the swollen feet, the irritations, the shopping for baby things, the learning as much as possible about children—all of these are stocked up with the stress of school and exams.

During the majority of my pregnancy, people are helpful; my fellow students and my instructors, but I've also heard rumors that I was hoeing around for money and that's how I got pregnant by accident. Because of what I have seen and felt with Alex, as well as the words that he has used for me, the rumors hurt me more than they should, actually. Consequently, I suffer from anxiety as a result of this.

Computer engineering has always been a complex course, but it feels harder being pregnant. Even with the pregnancy, I feel a renewed vigor to be my best, simply because I know that I need to do everything for my children so that they will be comfortable. I won't be able to stand on my own two feet if I give birth to them and then leave them to suffer. And while I know that there are good people out there, I will not give my children up for adoption. Instead, I will try my very best to raise them, take care of them, and give them everything they need. I won't watch them fail, so I have to be the best I can be.

I continue my part-time job in the coffee shop for a while. It isn't easy, but I need money more than ever. Maya is helping out, but I can't depend on her my whole life. She was quite angry when she found out that I was going to work again, but I convinced her that I had to do a lot so that I could make ends meet.

At six months pregnant, I can't continue anymore because I've gotten so big, the three children take up a lot of space, and I'm so easily drained. I don't have the strength to do anything at all; I just wanted to keep sleeping all day. I have to make myself study for my final exams to go into my senior year.

I tried my best to read as much as possible, while praying that I don't deliver during the exams, as my doctor said that multiple children are usually delivered before the expected date.

"Just be careful and don't stress yourself too much," Maya always says, and I get worried about her. She's always taking care of me, and I don't want her to fail her exams since she's focusing on me so much.

"I'll be fine, Maya; you take care of yourself," I say often, and she always laughs.

I manage to write all my papers without my water breaking or randomly giving birth. It's something for which I'm grateful for.

One day, I stand up as I feel a strong, sharp pain wrack across my stomach. "Aargh!" I exclaim. The cry barely left my mouth when Maya comes running to me.

"What is it?" "Are you okay?" she asks, and I try to calm myself and breathe in.

"I'm good, just a little pain," I say.

Maya glares at me. "We should go to the hospital; let the doctor check you out," she says, and I shake my head.

"It's not time yet," I argue. Maya said this when I had Braxton Hicks a few days ago. It seems like that's what is continuing, although I can note that the pain now is a bit more than the pain of the previous days.

"I just need to relax," I continue. Maya doesn't seem to believe me, but she nods and helps me lie down on the couch.

I must have been right, as I feel myself drifting into sleep. My babies aren't ready to show up, it seems.

Pain wakes me up from sleep this time, and it is a tad bit sharper than the last one. I wake up disoriented and trying to withhold the pain. I try to sit up on the couch, and I realize that my dress is wet. That could mean two things: either my water broke or I wet myself in my sleep. Considering the state of my bladder, the second option is actually plausible, but the first option seems more valid. It seems like my babies are coming after all.

I sit upright and try to remember every piece of information that I was told at the antenatal visit. One more sharp pain brings me back to reality, which is when I realize it is time to give birth. I stand up, clean up the sofa, and change into a new dress. Maya is sleeping, and I don't want to wake her up yet, so I walk around and arrange the babies' bags, and then I begin to time my contractions. As I move around, I feel two more, and by this time, they are thirty minutes apart. I wake Maya.

"Maya, I think we need to go to the hospital," I say. She stands up so quickly that you wouldn't be able to guess that she was sleeping.

I tell her, "I have already gotten everything ready; you should just get dressed," and although she appears to be a little confused, she nods her head in agreement.

She dresses quickly and then drives the both of us to the hospital. I know that I'm most probably going to do a CS, but I might still give birth vaginally. I'm ready for either option and can't wait to hold my babies in my arms.

Once we arrive, I'm dressed and examined by my physician. The contractions are coming fast now, and the pain is so strong that I can't calm down; I can't bear it.

"You will have to deliver vaginally," the doctor says, and I nod. I can't quantify the time that passes; only that I do a lot of screaming, then I scratch and push.

"You have a boy, my love, and there are two more to go," the doctor says after I'm done pushing out a baby. I'm so drained, but the screaming child gives me more hope than I could have ever imagined. I want all my babies. My first baby is clean, and I am allowed to hold him. He is still in my arms when another contraction wracks me; it's not yet over. Pushing this time requires more energy, and I know that the fact that I am already drained doesn't help.

"Here's the other boy; you are doing wonderfully; for a first mother, this is exceptional," the doctor compliments me as I smile at my second son. Having only myself and two children here makes me feel exhausted and drained. I can deal with two children; there is no need for a third one.

"Be strong, Julia; you'll be fine; just push for the third baby; it's your girl, Julia," Maya says, and I take a deep breath and gather my strength. I need to have my last baby; I can do it. With all my might, I push time and again until the doctor sees the head and is able to ease the body out of me.

"And it's a girl," the doctor announces, congratulating me. She's bloody, but she's positive and beaming. I'm allowed to hold my pretty girl for a little while before I push out the placenta and feel myself going into a deep sleep. I feel fulfilled, and even if I died today, I would feel like I accomplished a lot.

CHAPTER FIVE

JULIA

After four years of schooling, I manage to get my degree. Today is one of the best days of my life, and I can't even express how happy I am. I'm getting ready to go for my graduation ceremony, a year after I had my children, Luca, Landon, and Layla, who are turning one next week, and being a mother of three children still in diapers has been wonderful, to say the least.

I have only been able to take care of the children and also be the best in my class because Maya was there to help me; if not, I would still be struggling with my grades. As much as I loved and enjoyed my time as a college student, even with the ups and downs that came with it, I am so excited that I am finally done.

Alex's betrayal hurt me so much, but I have managed to move on from it. I haven't heard from him since I told him that I was pregnant. There were days when taking care of the triplets was difficult for me, and I would wish then that their father was with me and that he could help, but that wasn't to be. So, I accepted that, though I hated him for it. I still hate him.

Luca and Landon are already walking, but they're not yet steady on their feet, and Layla is unable to walk on her own just yet. That doesn't make her unable, though, to turn the entire house upside down. The triplets are a triple threat, as even this morning, I'm struggling to get dressed and to make sure that the kids didn't spoil something valuable before we left. I am putting on a red dress that ends at my knees but is pretty and simple. I pair the dress with low silver heels that will enable me to run around with my kids. I dressed all of them up in red; they have to twin with me today. It is incredibly difficult to take care of them alone, but Maya is also getting ready for her graduation, so I have to manage today. I want them to be present with me on my big day.

I put them in the car seat and the stroller into the trunk as I get ready to leave. As I get into the driver's seat, I'm so excited about how far I've come in life in general and so happy with the progress I've made. I got a part-time job in software engineering, and I was able to get a car on loan. As I have graduated, the job is now full-time, and I can work from home, which is best so that I can have time for my children.

The past year has been fair to me, as all that I have wanted I have been able to get.

"Julia!" Maya shouts when she sees me. I'm pushing the stroller that houses my three children, and I smile when I see her. The occasion hasn't started yet, but the place is already full of people wearing graduation gowns with smiles all over their faces. I'm so happy that I'm one of them and that I'm done. There were times when I felt so close to giving up, that I felt like I couldn't do it so there was no need to try.

"Maya!" I shout in response.

"Come, I saved seats for us in front," Maya says, and she leads me to the front of the hall. I go with the kids, and from there we watch as the procedures begin. I stand up, beaming with pride when my name is called to get my certificate. At that moment, I think of my parents and grandmother, and I hope I made them proud. I feel proud of myself, too, despite all odds. The applause from the crowd is massive. I was well known in my class as the girl who had triplets; just that was uncommon enough. Tears come down my face as I take my certificate. I'm so excited.

"I am so proud of you, honey," Maya says, hugging me tight when I come down from the stage. We have a family of our own. Her own family didn't come, as they're busy with business, so we are our own little family unit.

When it's Maya's turn, I shout loudly and cheer for her. The children are surprisingly excited and less cranky than I expected. I'm thinking of hiring a live-in nanny soon, as there is no way I can do it on my own.

"We did it, Julia. We got the degree!" Maya shouts when she comes down, and I smile at her.

Yes, we did it! "I am so happy!" I shout at her. There is no way I would have been able to do it on my own; if not for Maya, I probably would have dropped out.

"Thank you, Maya," I say sincerely, but my friend just shrugs.

"It's time for pictures!" she shouts, and we all go to snap shots of ourselves in our gowns, holding up our diplomas. We take pictures with the triplets, a few by ourselves, and that's it. I'm done with college, and I finished with three more parts of me than I came with—three children that I in no way expected—but I am done.

That night, after I put the kids to bed, I meet Maya in the living room, where she's watching TV.

"So, what's next?" she asks me, and I shrug.

"You've asked this question a million and one times, and my reply is still the same; I want to move on," I say. I don't want to remain in the States. The proximity of Alex is something that I can't handle. I want to move so far away that I can imagine that he doesn't exist or that he is dead; either way, I don't want to be close to him.

"Alexander is a bastard, and he is the one that is supposed to be running, not you. You don't have to leave the country just because of him," Maya says. Those have been her words from the very beginning. She has always wanted me to stay, but I have always wanted to leave. I haven't changed my mind yet, and I don't think I will.

"But I can travel; it's not like anything is really holding me here." I have the chance of leaving, so there's no reason for me not to. I can work from anywhere in the world. "I'm thinking of going to Australia," I say, and Maya shakes her head.

"So far away?" Maya asks, and I smile and nod. The further I go, the better. I want to start from scratch. I want to be close to Maya, as she is my closest friend and has helped me so much, but I feel like the only way I can truly move on is if I leave where Alex is. Start with a clean slate.

"I am so sorry, Maya," I say.

"Don't be. You should be able to move on. If this is what is best for you and your kids, then do it," Maya says. I feel bad for leaving her because of a man, but Alex isn't the only reason I want to move. The looks that I get, from being a good and simple girl to being a mother of three without a baby daddy coming around, the gossip. When my kids grow up, the toxicity might be transferred to them. I don't want that to happen, so I will protect my children, and if a new country is best, I will move there.

"When will you leave?" Maya asks and sighs. We have had this discussion previously, but they were all arguments about why I shouldn't go. This is the only time that Maya is actually accepting the fact that I will leave. I hate to hurt her, but I have to. I have to leave. This is also for her. The usual extrovert party girl I met has diminished ever since I got pregnant. She had become a mother just like me, and I hate that I had such an impact on her life. I want her to have her life back; if I go to another country, she won't feel so obligated to take care of me and the kids. I'll take care of my children with the help of a nanny.

"As soon as possible, Maya." I'd already started the visa process. "Flight tickets will come next," I say, and Maya sighs and moves closer to me.

"I will miss you, Julia," she says, hugging me tight. I don't want to leave her either, and tears sting my eyes. I try not to cry, because I have to comfort her since I am the one who chose to leave.

"We still have time to spend together; I'm not going just yet." Maya nods at this.

"We're going to spend your last days together. Oh my God, my children; I'm not going to watch them grow. You have to come to visit as much as possible, and I will do the same. We will find ways to see each other as often as possible." Maya friend clearly understands how little we will see of each other once we leave. My plan isn't to come back as often as possible; I actually plan not to come at all, maybe once every two years, but with time, we will grow apart, and I want another life with my children.

"You sound like I am going to die, Maya. We're still going to talk on the phone, and we will facetime each other. I'm not going off the face of the earth," I joke, just to relieve the tension in the air.

"Yes, yes, but the more physical the better," Maya says, and I can't help but laugh.

As planned, we spent the last month in each other's company. Maya, the kids, and I went everywhere together. We went to amusement parks and restaurants, spending as much time together as possible. We were just two friends who found it hard to let go.

When the dreaded time to leave drew nearer and nearer, Maya helped me pack all my belongings in trunks and got me ready to leave. She helped me with everything that I needed in Australia and then drove us to the airport.

"I will miss you all so much," Maya says with tears in her eyes. She hugs me so hard, and I can't hold back my own tears. My friend, whom I have known for so long, is now leaving me all alone. Technically, I'm the one leaving her, but the result is the same nonetheless.

"I will miss you so much, Maya," I say. I know that it will be almost impossible to find a friend who is so true and who is so selfless enough to care for my kids and me for such a long time. She is even more than family to me.

"Stay in touch," Maya says, and I walk down the aisle to the plane. I nod my head at her. I will stay in touch, I will not be able to do without my friend.

I take the stroller onto the plane, and with the help of the air hostess, the kids are strapped in, and we are ready to leave.

The plane starts moving, and I know that it is truly a new beginning for me and my children, away from their father and away from everything else. I cannot wait to begin this new life with Landon, Luca, and Layla.

***

Five years later

"I have great news, Julia." I'm sitting in my living room at home in Australia. The house is larger and more sophisticated than anything I have ever owned. A few years ago, I would have never believed that this property could be mine. I'm talking to Maya over the phone. We have been in constant communication over the years, and as I had predicted, she got into a relationship right after I left. She is happier, which I can confirm, so I know I made a good decision on that part.

"What is it?" I ask. I am ecstatic to know what it is. Our communication hadn't diminished with time, and Maya had come three times to see us in Australia; the kids even knew her as Aunt Maya. They love their godmother, even if they don't get to see her very often.

"Raymond proposed." Raymond was the guy Maya had been with for the past two years. different from the man that she first dated when the kids and I first left the States.

"Really?" I ask. I'm already so excited for her. This is wonderful news.

"Yes, truly. The ring is so beautiful. I'll send you a picture. It was last night while we were at the park when he popped the question. I'm so happy, I feel like I could burst," Maya says, and I let out a scream. I am so happy for her. I could tell from the way she spoke about him that she loved him. As long as she loved him, I wanted her to marry him. I want happiness for my friend; she deserves it.

"I am so happy for you, Maya. You deserve this. "

"Thank you, Julia." The wedding is in two months, and we are having a small ceremony in the Bahamas. It is a chance to get away for both of us. I know this is a lot to ask, but I want you to be there. I want you to witness my happiest moment; I don't want to do this alone," Maya says, and I shake my head.

"The hell, Maya?" Are you pleading with me to come to your wedding? I would go to Mars if you were getting married there. It is your wedding, Maya. I will do anything for you; you have done too much for me and the kids for me to miss your wedding," I say to my friend. I can hear sniffles from the other side of the line.

"Are you crying?" I ask, and Maya sniffles even more.

"I'm not crying; it's a bit windy over here," she says, and I laugh.

"I know that you're most likely in your room," I say, and she laughs out loud.

"Landon, Luca, Layla, and I will be in the Bahamas waiting for you," I say, and she laughs again.

"I'm the one getting married; you guys don't have to be there before me," she says.

"Anything for our godmother. You had better have spots for all of us in your wedding party," I threaten.

"Oh, oh, I forgot." I haven't asked you. Julia, please, will you be my maid of honor?" she asks, and I laugh again.

"Do you really have to ask?" Of course, I already know that's my job, I will be annoyed if you ask anyone else to do it," I say.

"Okay, okay. Good. "So, can Landon and Luca be the ring bearers and Layla the flower girl?" she asks, and I sigh.

"Those children are yours, Maya; use them as you see fit," I say.

"I am so excited, Julia. "I am actually getting married!" Maya screams, and I smile again. I want to be close to her so that I can hug her tight, but she is too far away.

"Yes, love. "It seems like you both have everything planned out, you already had a venue and dates," I say. Maya laughs sheepishly.

"Well, I have always wanted to go to the Bahamas, and Raymond said we can get married there when he proposed, and he also said he wants us to get married as soon as possible, so we ended up picking two months. The major details haven't been made yet," Maya says.

"I can't wait to be there with the kids, to see you again, and to finally meet Raymond in person. I am sad that I won't be around to help plan the wedding, though.

"That isn't an issue at all. I'm going to hire an event planner and literally leave everything to her; I want a simple wedding," Maya says. One thing that I realized is that even after I left, Maya didn't revert to the party girl she'd been before I got pregnant. The Maya I knew before wouldn't want a simple wedding. The more extravagant, the better. I don't know if I should say she is maturing or if I should be worried about her.

"You want a simple wedding, Maya?" I ask. I can barely believe my ears.

"Would I be getting married in the Bahamas if I didn't want a simple wedding?" she asks, and I think about it. The location makes sense for a simple wedding, yet I know that it won't be simple. Maybe I don't understand her own definition of "simple."

"There's no problem, Maya; I'll be there to support you. Just go on and make babies so that I have godchildren too," I say with a laugh.

"You already have three children, Julia, why do you want more?" Maya asks with a laugh.

"Not more children; I want godchildren, the ones that I see once in a while and who give kisses and gifts here and there. I don't have to stay with them all day," I say, and Maya laughs.

That's one definition. Alright, no problem; I'll make you godchildren, but just one at a time. You have enough multiple births for both of us," Maya says. I hear some distractions from the phone, and I can deduce that someone is calling Maya.

"I have to go. I'll talk to you and the kids later," she says before she ends the call.

"Yes, later," I say. I look at the time and realize it's almost time to get the children from kindergarten. They started attending school when they turned five. Since then, I've had a lot of free time. I'm even thinking of getting a day job just to keep myself from getting bored, but I also know that I may regret my choice.

The children are ready to leave as soon as I get to the school. I see Luca and Landon first and I am reminded of Alex. They look so much like him that it drives me crazy. The older they grow, the more they resemble their father. Layla looks like Alex too, but at least she has my lips; none of them have my hair. I left the States to avoid Alex, but he followed me to Australia.

"Mom!" the children shout as they run to me. They just turned six a week ago, but they are still very much a handful. I hug them all and kiss their heads.

"Hey, guys. How was school today? I ask as we walk to my car. Landon and Layla begin to chat immediately about their teacher and what they did. Luca is the only one who is quiet, as usual. Even if my middle child looks nothing like me, his temperament reminds me of myself. how quiet he is and how he holds himself.

"That is all very nice. We are going on vacation, guys," I announce, and the children start hooting, especially Landon and Layla.

"Where are we going, Mom?" Luca asks first.

"Yes, Mom, where are we going?" Landon asks.

"Where are we going?" Layla parrots them, and I feel like this will turn into an argument.

"Stop saying what I said." This was Landon. It's funny that he would say that since he copied Luca.

"I didn't, I said, where are we going? You said, 'Mom, where are we going?'" Layla says smartly, and I smile. Smart girl.

"That is the same thing," Landon says. I know that it's already going to turn into a full-blown fight, so I try to avoid it.

"We're going to the Bahamas!"

"Babamas?" Layla asks.

"Pajamas?" This time it's Landon.

"Where is that?" Luca asks.

"Well, it's an island surrounded by water, and it's a gorgeous place. We are going to a wedding."

"Oh, are you getting married, Mom?" Landon asks, and I almost laugh out loud.

"Are we getting a dad now?" Layla asks this time. And I'm shocked and try to stabilize myself.

"I am not getting married. Aunt Maya is getting married." I almost want to close my eyes. I remember being in that room when Alex denied his children. When he laughed when I told him that he was the only man that I had been with.

"Aunt Maya! We are going to see Aunt Maya!" Layla shouts.

"Aunt Maya is getting married." Landon says it calmly. They forgot about getting a father for a little while. I have to think of what to tell them. I hate Alex; he is putting me through so much.

CHAPTER SIX

JULIA

The air in the Bahamas is warm, and the weather is simply to die for. The entire vacation is something that I knew I would enjoy.

I get here with the kids a bit earlier than expected, and Maya and Raymond have not checked into the hotel yet.

"Mom, this place is so cool!" Landon says as we walk into the hotel. The children are so excited to be in another country, and they are portraying their excitement in full force, even Luca.

"Mom, is there a swimming pool?" Layla asks, and I almost feel like rolling my eyes. I have no idea where all the questions are coming from. They're just hitting me left, right, and center with questions. They want to ask everything all at once; they want to know everything, and I don't even have all the answers to give them.

"Yes, Layla, there is a swimming pool," Ariana, the young nanny that is helping me take care of the children, says. I know that it will be very difficult to do my bridesmaid duties with the children running all around, which is why I convinced Ariana to come with us. She is excited, of course. It's an all-expenses-paid trip to a place that she previously hasn't been to. So, she had taken the offer. The twenty-one year old nanny reminds me of myself when I was younger and willing to do anything to be successful. Now, twenty-eight seems way too old, too ancient, to be having childish wiles.

"Oh, Ms. Arianna, can we swim, please?" Landon asks, and I smile. Their enthusiasm is so infectious.

"You have to ask your mom, I am afraid," Ariana says. The children are already used to Ariana; she has been their nanny for close to a year now. She does her job well and is marvelous with children, even if she is very young. The children's previous nanny had been an older lady, more like a grandmother to the children. They loved her to bits, but she'd had to retire.

"Mom, can we go swimming?" Luca asks. I have a soft spot for Luca, and that's something I can admit. I like to say that it's because he doesn't ask often. Sometimes I feel inclined to do exactly what he wants when he asks, but I know that it's more that he acts a lot like me, and that is enough reason.

"Only if you are under supervision and with floaties, too," I say. The children can swim fairly well, but I won't let them out of my sight. It's too easy to drown, and while it feels at times that the children are too much for me to handle, I can't deal with any of them getting hurt.

"Yay!" they all shout, jumping around. I just smile at them. We all walk to our suite and settle in. We're still settling down when Maya calls me, and I know that she must have arrived.

"Are you here yet?" I ask immediately when I pick up the call.

"Yes, love, we are here," Maya says, and I smile.

"Alright, what is your room number? The kids and I will be there in a jiffy," I say. Maya gives me their room number before she disconnects the call.

"Okay, kids, let's get ready, we're going to see Aunt Maya," I say. As expected, my children jump up and are ready to get dressed.

Ariana and I help them get ready, and we go up to Maya's room. It is a penthouse at the resort. From what little I know of Raymond, he always goes for the best, especially for Maya. He likes quality things, and he loves my friend, which is a good thing.

Maya opens the door after we knock, and she squeals as she sees the children.

"Landon, Layla, Luca!" Maya shouts, and the children run to hug her. They are all excited to see her. She gathers them up and kisses them as they embrace her in return. I am reminded of when I had just given birth to the triplets and Maya was carrying them. She loves my children so much that I feel guilty for keeping them from her for this long.

"Julia," Raymond says. He's even more handsome in person than in the pictures Maya sent. He is tall and exudes power, just like Alex. I shake every thought of Alex from my mind. I don't need to be thinking about him at all. He's not worthy of my thoughts.

"Raymond," I say, shaking the hand he extends. He has a warm smile on his face that reminds me that he is still very human. In my mind, it separates me from Alex, because Raymond is human and a man in love.

"She loves them a lot, doesn't she?" Raymond asks. I look at him, and

I can see the admiration in his eyes that he has for my friend. He loves her very much. Not many men would understand the relationship between Maya and me, but he does, and he respects it. This is something that I can love.

"She does," I say. "I love them too, but they are my babies," I continue, and I laugh. Maya is so engrossed in her conversation with the kids that I'm not even certain she saw me.

"You both should come in," Raymond says, referring to Ariana and me. Ariana looks skeptical but comes in reluctantly.

We both sit down in the living room, and Maya is gifting the children with chocolate and other things. They all seem excited about all their gifts. After Maya is done spoiling them, they run to me.

"Mom, see what Aunt Maya gave me!" Landon says. He's usually the first to talk; he has so much confidence, and that is something I admire. Even Layla, who is the same age as Landon, admires her big brother, even if they are always at loggerheads.

"I can see it, Landon; it is very nice. You want to take it home and show it to your friends?" I ask my son, and he nods quickly with a huge smile on his face.

"Aunt Maya gave me gifts too," Layla pipes up.

"Yes, dear, I can see that very well; all your gifts are very pretty," I say to my children. They seemed satisfied by this. Luca is studying his toy intently, and I know that he is already thinking about how he wants to disassemble it and then possibly put it back together. It is a habit that Luca has that I find hard to curb because, if I am being honest, I like the way his mind works.

"Julia," Maya says, and I stand up from my chair and walk to my friend. She looks happy, and she is glowing like a bride is supposed to. It's almost like she is radiating all the love that she is feeling. I love that she is happy; I want her to be for as long as she lives. For all she has done for me, she doesn't need one minute of sadness.

"Maya, you look so beautiful; love looks good on you," I say.

"Do you mean it? I feel good, actually. I feel like I could be floating from all the happiness that I'm feeling," she says, touching her face.

"The happiness is showing for sure," I say. For a minute, I'm jealous of how happy she is, but just for a minute, because I know that she deserves it, and more. But for that moment, I want to be her. I want to glow in happiness and be throwing side glances at the man that I love. I want to be so excited to get married. I want to live together forever with a man who will love me just like I love him. The only issue is the fact that I am scared, and I am afraid that the next person I get close to will be like Alex. Not that I allow many men to get close, though, because the children scare them. They can't take care of three children that aren't theirs.

"That is so nice. I am a bit nervous, though. It's so hard to imagine that by tomorrow I will be a married woman. I'm afraid to get married; I love Raymond, but what are these cold feet? The ceremony itself is scaring me at this point," Maya says, and I shake my head.

"Don't worry about it so much. You love this man, and he loves you; therefore, everything will work out well. It is just you being nervous, and that is okay," I say, and she smiles.

"Can you stay with me tonight?" We can have our own bridal shower. I didn't have one back home. My family will fly in this evening, as will my sisters, and some of my coworkers will come, but it will be mostly you and me. They want me to have a bridal shower, but I won't totally mind it if you are with me," Maya says, and I smile.

"You should know that you don't have to ask me these things; just drag me here and I am in," I say, and she laughs.

Raymond moves out of the hotel room, as the penthouse is for the bridal shower. Ariana is sleeping with the children in my room. Maya's friends, her siblings, and her cousins come for the shower, and come well prepared. I'm barely doing any work. I just stay close to my friend and walk her through the process. We're having so much fun. Maya's friends are really nice people, and I'm enjoying my time with them as well. I'm starting to wonder if I'd do something like that if I ever got married. I know that I won't marry, though; it's not sensible for a single mother of three to wish for marriage. It's best to just focus on caring for my children, and that's what I am doing. There's no need to bother myself with thoughts of love and marriage; they're all irrelevant.

The wedding was yesterday morning, and it was beautiful. It was a beach wedding, and I should have questioned Maya when she said that she wanted a small wedding. It was anything but small. If one thousand guests were able to come to the Bahamas, they would have. Maya's family all showed up for her, and the hotel was booked full. The decor of the wedding was beautiful and calm, and maybe that was what Maya meant by a simple wedding. There were at least three hundred guests in attendance, which was huge given that the ceremony was on a beach. The reception happened in a hall, and it was beautiful.

Maya was a blushing bride. I helped her arrange her dress and helped with her makeup. I took care of her and did everything that had to be done. Ariana was wonderful with the children and sat by them as they performed their various duties. But by the end of the day, I was exhausted. The wedding was a success, though, and that was the main thing. I was so happy for my friend.

Raymond and Maya are staying on the island for their honeymoon. I'm also staying with the kids for a few more days just so that the sun will touch our skin and we will feel fresh before we go back home.

The children are excited about staying, even if it was already planned. Ariana is excited too. She's happy and content, playing with the children on the beach and all around.

Two days after the wedding, all the guests have already checked out of the hotel. Ariana, Landon, Luca, Layla, and I are at the beach to enjoy the sun and play.

"Don't go too far, Landon," I shout to my son as he runs with a ball. As I shout, Luca suddenly feels fortified lying under the shade with me and goes out to play ball with his brother.

"I will go bring them closer," Ariana says as she stands up, but I hold out a hand to her.

"Don't worry, they won't go too far," I say. Layla is lying by Ariana's side and watching her brothers as they play. At first, I knew that Layla would only stay back because Landon was the only one playing and she didn't want to be bad, but now that Luca is playing, she is contemplating what she will do.

"You can go play, Layla," I say, and my daughter stands up from the mat like lightning and begins to play with her brothers. It's almost like she's beating them at their own game immediately after joining.

They are playing when Luca throws the ball far, and it hits an umbrella. I let out a screech as I see an elderly woman lying down under the umbrella. I stand up immediately to go and apologize to her. I know that it is a beach ball and will most probably not hurt, but I also know that she is an old woman. I'm just hoping that no bones have been broken.

The children walk with me as I go to the tent; all looking solemn, most especially Luca. Knowing my middle son, it will be a while before he touches a ball again.

The ball that hit the older lady's umbrella threw her off balance.

"I am so sorry for the ball, ma'am; my children were playing and the ball hit your umbrella," I say to the old lady, and I give my children the look to tell them to apologize.

"We are sorry for the ball, ma'am," they all say in unison, almost like they'd practiced it. When my children do this, I can almost bet that they have psychic communication and connection.

"Oh, it's alright, my love," the old lady says with a smile. She is looking at my children so intently that it's almost like she has met them before; maybe she was at the wedding.

But when she speaks, the voice sounds familiar, as though I've already met her somewhere.

"Your children are very beautiful. Did you come from the States to attend the wedding at the hotel?" she asks, and I smile. That was where she knew the kids from, I guess, the wedding.

"We came for the wedding, yes; Maya is my friend, but we are not from the States; we live in Australia," I say, and she smiles. I like the aura that the old lady is exuding; it's one of importance. She is clearly someone who has power. Her white hair is flowing down her shoulders, and she is wearing a flower-print blue gown with spaghetti straps. She looks like she's in her late sixties, but I wouldn't be surprised to find out if she is much older because people like that tend to take good care of their bodies.

"Oh, Australia. I've been there a few times; it is a beautiful country," she says, and I smile.

"I'm Olivia Parker," she says, stretching her hand to mine. Even the way she holds her hand speaks of affluence and wealth.

"My name is Julia Anderson; these are my children," I say, and she smiles.

"What are your names?" she asks the children, and they seem excited to engage.

"I am Landon Anderson."

"I am Luca Anderson."

"I am Layla Anderson."

They all chime in, "And we are six years old," and Olivia grins and claps her hands as if she is delighted by their announcement.

"Six is such a big age," she says, and they smile.

"I will be seven next year," Landon adds. perhaps to seem even older.

"We will all be seven next year," Layla pipes in, and I smile. They are so good at antagonizing each other; it's cute to watch.

"And on the same day, too," Luca adds, and I am surprised at this one. Luca barely adds in when Landon and Layla are at their wordplay.

"Exactly!" Layla says it with increased fervor. She is clearly excited to have someone on her side.

"How old are you?" Luca asks Olivia, and I am too shocked that my son actually asked the question, let alone even saying anything.

"Oh, that is a very big number," Olivia says. I smile at her response; she seems to be good with kids.

"I know very big numbers," Luca counters. I shrug then; he does know big numbers. Luca was ahead of his siblings a bit in the academic scheme of things.

"I am seventy-five," she says, and all the children gasp.

"That is a very big number," Luca agrees, and Olivia nods again.

"I am really sorry for all these questions, Olivia, we should go on and play; let's not disturb your leisure time," I say. I feel a bit ashamed that my kids are asking a complete stranger so many questions at once.

"Oh, don't worry; they are almost like my own great-grandchildren. I don't mind, it brings me peace," Olivia says, and I am surprised but I nod.

"Sit down, children," Olivia says, and the children sit on the mat.

"You have great-grandchildren this age?" I ask her. It seems farfetched, even at her age.

"Oh yes, my granddaughter has a child already; I'm just waiting on my grandsons," she says, and I nod in surprise.

"Wow!"

For the rest of our time at the beach, the children stay with Nana Olivia because that is what her great-granddaughter calls her. They enjoy themselves and don't even want to leave when it is time to go. I exchanged contact information with Olivia, and all in all, it's an exciting vacation.

CHAPTER SEVEN

OLIVIA

I can barely conceal my excitement when I get back to the States. I don't know what I stumbled on during my stay in the Bahamas, but something tells me that it is very important. I know that the triplets are Alexander's children; it is very obvious from their looks. They are identical to their father. It is such a shame that they are not with him.

I don't know what transpired between him and Julia, but I know that I owe it to them to fix it so that their family unit can be complete and my great-grandchildren will not grow up without a father.

I did a little research on Julia Anderson, the woman who most probably had a fling with my grandson. She is very simple and delicate, and I know that Alex would have done something very wrong. He's quite cynical these days, and the woman he is with doesn't help matters.

According to the private investigator, Julia was a student here in the States until five years ago. She delivered all her children here and left their father's name blank on the birth certificate. The report also listed Maya as her very close friend. Doing a quick run on Maya, the sweet lady who got married, I realized that she was once in a relationship with Calvin, Alex's friend, around the time that Julia would have gotten pregnant, and that was the relationship I was searching for. The signs were already leading; presumably that is how they met.

I do not think Alex is aware of the existence of his children; if he were, he would have never agreed to the marriage of convenience he was about to have with Jocelyn. I am very worried about my grandson. Before he agreed to the contract marriage that will help boost his company, he was just playing the field, and as far as I know, he's still playing the field, and that happened after Genevieve betrayed him. He caught the girl in bed with his so-called best friend. He was deeply wounded then; at least I know that very well. I felt terrible for my grandson, but there was nothing I could do.

I can do something now though. I sense that there should be some sort of attraction between the two of them before they had three children together. A marriage of attraction is far better than a marriage of convenience. Jocelyn is too cold for my liking; one would wonder if she were a doll rather than a human.

I am impatiently waiting for the DNA test that I sent out yesterday. I secretly took samples from the kids when I was with them, and getting them from Alex was easy. All I had to do was trick him into bringing me soup on the pretense that I was sick. Now all I need to do is place them in the same room together; everything else will work out on its own after that.

The major problem is how to get Julia and the triplets back to the US. I can't just call her and ask her to come, can I? I have to first look to see if she has any family that links her here or something that can pressure her to come back home, even if it's just for a weekend.

***

JULIA

I rush to my phone as soon as I hear it ring. It's late at night, and I just finished working on a code. My work is rather enjoyable since it gives my children and me a comfortable life. I get to work my own hours, too, so I have enough time to spend with my children. The triplets are asleep, and it is the best time for me to work. It's been two weeks since we came back from the Bahamas, and home has felt a little bit dreary. Seeing Maya fall in love has made me long for love, too. I want what my friend has: a chance to fall in love and to have a complete family unit. While I love my children to bits and would trade anything and everything I have for them, I still long for the love of a man. I didn't know that I still had these feelings, at least not before now, before seeing my friend so happy, so the itch to have someone of my own has increased. It doesn't help that I hadn't been with anyone before Alex, and even after Alex, there has been no one else. There have been friends and those who actually wanted something to happen, but there has been no one who lasted long enough for me to form a love interest.

"Hello," I say as I pick up the call, removing all thoughts of love from my mind. The number is a foreign one that I don't recognize, and for a while I don't know who's calling me or the reason for the call.

"Hello, Julia. It is me, Olivia. We met at the beach the other day," she says, and I smile and nod in remembrance. I would have recognized her voice even if she hadn't introduced herself.

"Olivia. How have you been? It has been a while," I say, sitting down on the chair and getting more relaxed. The children love the older lady, and they were all over her before we left the beach together. She even made me promise to visit anytime I was in the States.

"I actually haven't been very good, Julia. I've been quite down for the past few days. How are the triplets? My little great-grandchildren—I hope they're doing fine? I am missing them already," she says, and I frown. Even if she tried to sway away from what she started with, I know that she isn't feeling very well, and I don't want her to be sick at all. I'm already worried for her.

"Oh, what's wrong with you, Olivia? The children are fine, and they miss you, too. Are you at the hospital?" I ask her. The children did miss her very much; they couldn't stop talking about her. She was their Nana, and they loved her to bits, even if they only knew her for a while.

"I'm just a bit sick, but I'm taking my medication at home. I am excited that the children miss me; I miss them very much, and I miss you too," Olivia says, and I smile. The older lady is so nice to my children and me. I feel such a bond with her that it will be extremely hard to break. I enjoyed the time that we had together while we were in the Bahamas.

Oh, that is so nice. Just take your medication and make sure your children are around you," I say. I have a feeling that she misses her family. The way she talked about her children and her grandchildren, it was almost like she didn't spend enough time with them, and she wanted to change all that.

"It's not that easy, Julia. I feel like my time is almost up. It's almost like life is just disappearing through my fingers right in front of me. My sickness isn't one that is physical; it's more mental," she says, and I am truly shocked. The impression that I had of Olivia was that she was a very happy woman; she didn't seem like someone who was dealing with depression or anything like that. I am so hurt that she is hurt; I want her to be okay immediately. I don't want her to feel bad or in pain at all.

"You shouldn't feel like that, Olivia. There is so much in life to enjoy; you have your family, and you still have more years. You should watch your great-grandchildren grow," I say, and I feel like crying now.

"Thank you, Julia." I will try my best. "There is something that I want, though," Olivia says, sniffling just a little. My ears are perked because I want to hear what she has to say. I have a feeling that it will be something important.

"What is it?" I ask immediately.

"I know that this is too much to ask, but I feel like I will go any day now, and I want to see the children at least once before I go. I don't know if you can come to the States for a quick visit, but you shouldn't worry about all the expenses. I will take care of all the finances," Olivia says, and I'm shocked to say the least. That was the last thing I expected her to say. This is too much to ask of someone who is basically a stranger, but I know that she is an old lady, and these kinds of thoughts are not so absurd for older people.

"I don't think I will be able to come to the States, Olivia. I am sorry," I say, and the other end of the line is silent for a while.

"Please, Julia. I want to see the children one last time; one day will be enough. An old woman is begging you." My heart aches for her, and I don't know how to say no to her. She's a sick old woman, and saying no would make me feel terrible. Would one weekend really change anything? I should try to move on from Alex; I can't avoid the States all my life.

I begin considering leaving and going to see Olivia a few minutes after saying no to the lady; she is already changing my mind.

I open my mouth to tell her no again, that it wasn't possible, and I don't want the children to get too attached to her, that I can't clear my schedule, and that I don't want the children to miss too much school. The children can't take that amount of travel in one month. Yet, I can't say anything; I'm stuck for a moment; the words won't leave me. I can't say no to her; I know that. The children will be excited to see her. They might even be angry if they find out that I said no to their great-grandmother.

"I will come, but not until next weekend," I say finally.

"Oh, thank you so much, Julia. I will be expecting you then!" Her voice is so sharp now—a far cry from how calm it was when she was telling me to come over. I take it as a sign that she is excited for the time that we will spend together.

"Yes, I will inform the children; I am sure they will be very excited to come," I say. I can already imagine their excitement when I let them know that we are going to the States. They will be so happy.

"That's nice. I will start getting ready for when you arrive," she says.

"Don't worry yourself, Olivia." Focus on getting yourself better. "We don't need too much; we just want to see you healthy and strong," I say. That's enough to calm her down.

"I will be calm. Thank you very much."

Everything will be fine; I will not see Alex, I tell myself after the call is over, trying to convince myself that I made the right decision by going to the States with the children.

California is a huge state; I might not even be close to where Alex is. He won't see me, and, most importantly, I will never see him. I don't want to see him at all. I'm not sure I'd be okay if I was in close proximity to him. But I realize now, after all these years, I have to do it, though, to at least get some form of closure.

***

"You are going where?" Leo asks. The next morning, I'm already getting ready to go to the States. I've told the children about the trip, and they're so excited to see Nana Olivia.

"I'm going to California," I simply say to my friend and neighbor of the past few years. I had wanted to live a simple life in Australia. I just wanted to have a simple family with my children. I wanted to take them to school, come back home, work, and not be involved with anything at all. I didn't want to make friends with or date men, but the men came. They usually scared my children, but they came. The friends also came, even if they were just coparents and, in this case, my hot neighbor.

When I first met Leo, I still hated the entire male species, except my boys. I didn't give him any mind. But after a year or so, I began to develop crush on him. It wasn't something that I planned at all; it just happened, and the fact that I could care for someone again meant that I wasn't completely broken. The crush was something that shouldn't have happened, as Leo obviously didn't feel the same. Even when I desperately tried to show him the signs that I liked him, he didn't show any interest at all, and at one point, I began to wonder if he was scared of my children, too; only he loved them as much as one would love their own children, and my kids adored Uncle Leo. He's the closest thing they had to a father figure.

He knows so much about me, as one couldn't spend years with another person and not spill a few secrets or ten, and so it was understandable that he reacted with shock when I told him that I was going back to the state that I left because of trauma.

"You don't want to go back there; you've said this over and over again that you don't want reminders of what happened to you while you were there; you came to Australia for that very reason, so why do you want to go now?" he asks me, and I shrug.

"We met an old lady while we were in the Bahamas; I believe I told you about her, Olivia. She's sick, and she wants to see the kids one last time; I will not deny an old woman her dying wish," I say, and Leo scoffs.

"This seems rather fishy. How does an old lady suddenly meet you and the kids and a few weeks later you are the ones she wants to see before she dies?" Leo says it skeptically, but I shrug again. "What happened to your reasoning that you wouldn't be able to go back to the States?" Leo asks. I don't like that he's questioning me, but then again, I know that he's my friend and that he wants the best for me. He doesn't want me to be hurt.

"I think I need some closure. I can't run away from the area where he lives all my life. I don't want to meet him or do anything odd like that; I just want to be able to walk down the streets of California without being scared if I see him. I shouldn't be afraid to see him, and I shouldn't be running from him. I did nothing wrong, so I think I will go, just to prove that I can.

"I don't know, Julia; you're doing just fine here. I don't think that you need closure, and I don't like the idea of you breaking down again. You don't have to risk all that for a woman you barely know," Leo says, and I sigh.

"I'll be fine, Leo. I'm strong, so I'll be fine. I can walk past him and say nothing. Besides, it has been a while, and California is still home. By next week-end, Maya will be back there, and when I go to her house, we can have a little time together, so it's all good. I can even visit my alma mater if I want. I can go to the coffee shop where I once worked. Alex isn't the only one in the States. "It has been a long time, and it's good if I visit," I say. I'm trying to convince myself as much as Leo. The children's excitement is enough reason for me to accept the invitation, but if I was going just for myself, there were a lot of other reasons, too.

"Yes, you are right. I just worry for you, Julia. You just have to be safe when you're there, and if you call me, I'll be with you in a minute; you don't have to explain; I'll be on the next plane," Leo says, and I know that he is serious. He'd do a lot for me; he just won't take me as a love interest. It's really so sad.

"Thank you, Leo," I say before I continue packing.

The next weekend, I get ready with the children to fly again, this time to the same place that we flew from five years ago. I called Olivia before I left, and she sent me her address, which I can easily get to. A few days before my trip, I started to wonder if I knew Olivia before. She kept giving me the vibe of someone that I had met previously or knew. I can't shake the thoughts, though; they keep coming back like pestering flies. The entire ride gives me a nostalgic feeling, and I remember all the feelings I felt when I was leaving the States. I felt like my life had been thrown off balance; it was hard for me to focus on anything, so I had to leave. I only managed to stay until I completed my degree, and after that, I couldn't do it anymore.

I left with unhappiness because I knew that I was leaving my only friend behind. This time, though, I am going back to meet a friend, albeit a new one. I'm a lot more accomplished than I was the last time. I own a house and a car. I'm able to take care of my children and send them to school, and that is enough for me. The hurt feeling I felt five years ago is gone; I don't feel anything for Alex anymore, at least that's what I've told myself over the years. I have tried to rationalize what he did, that maybe he had a reason for behaving in that manner, and whichever solution I came up with, I was still angry with him.

The anger has lessened now; it has numbed. But I'm not happy with him, and if I see him, I may strangle him, but I don't spend hours thinking of him. I don't spend days wishing that things worked out between us. I don't try to stalk him anymore to know what he is doing or if he has moved on with another woman. I'm not interested in knowing if he has children or if he is still a womanizer. So many things have changed in the past five years; most of all, I've grown and am was wiser now at twenty-eight.

CHAPTER EIGHT

JULIA

California isn't much different than when I left. There isn't much of a culture shock, just nostalgia. I feel like I'm thinking too much as the driver that Olivia sent comes and drives us to her residence. The children are convinced that we are going to some castle where their Nana Olivia is the queen or something. They've made it into some sort of adventure, and Landon is clearly the leader; he enjoys things like that. The children's joy is the only thing that distracts me from my thoughts. I just keep thinking about how things could go wrong. After my conversation with Leo, I feel like something bad will happen on my trip. I'm still slightly scared that I may run into Alexander.

Olivia Parker's home is simply a mansion; that is the simplest way to put it. The house is bigger than anything I have ever seen in real life. It looks more like a palace that belongs to those who are royalty, unlike a house where regular people live. It is so big that it can house a hundred people. I'm wondering what kind of money she has that she can afford to live in such grandeur.

"It is a palace!" Layla exclaims as the car moves into the compound. I can agree with my daughter that it is a palace; if it could be called more than a palace, then the name would still be fitting.

"Yes, love," I say. "It is very big." I'm at a loss for words, because I'm still in awe of the grandeur. I would have expected something simple, but then again, with the way the lady carried herself, I knew that she had influence. But this was out of this world.

"Does Nana Olivia live here?" Luca asks. He is clearly as shocked as I am.

"Yes, she does," I say. I'm beginning to wonder at this point if she is secretly royalty, and that is why she exuded an aura of importance.

"Welcome, welcome," Olivia says as we come out of the car. She is looking as virile and healthy as the last time we saw her. I can even say that she is glowing this time. The smile on her face, the way that she walks toward us, I wonder why she called us to her when she is clearly not sick. The children don't seem to care about that at all, as they all run to her immediately.

"Nana Olivia!" they shout, and she hugs them closely. They're having little conversations together as she holds them close and even sings to them. All my inhibitions and questions fly out the window as I watch the way she is with the children. They clearly love her, and she loves them as well, and that is enough for me.

"Come in, Julia." Let me show you around," Olivia says, threading her hand through mine. The children are on either side of us, tugging on us to hurry in. They want to see the castle.

"Are you a queen?" Layla asks.

Olivia laughs. "No, honey, I'm not," she says.

"How come you live in a castle, then?"

"It's not a palace, honey. It's just a big house."

"Wow! I've never seen anything like this before. This big house is amazing.

"So how was your trip?" Olivia asks.

"It was great. The kids love being on a plane, and I don't mind it either.

"That's wonderful, then. Maybe I'll see you guys more often from now on. I guess now isn't the right time to tell her how difficult this trip was for me. how I kept overthinking my decision again and again.

"I can see that you are well now," I say and raise an eyebrow at her. She has the goodwill to blush. I don't know why she is doing all of this, but I strangely feel safe with her. I know that she won't hurt me or my children. So I play along with her for a while. Going with the flow seems like the easiest thing to do, and it is even a little fun.

"Oh yes, I am actually better. I am so happy now that the children are around. I actually do have something to tell you, but I will talk to you later about it." She looks serious about it, and I know that it is probably the reason she made me come to the States with the children. My curiosity is piqued, but she doesn't seem to be ready to share right now. The children are so excited to be shown around the house that they won't even let Olivia go for a moment.

The tour is very nice and insightful. I walk around, exploring various parts of the huge house. The place is actually out of this world.

"My husband was actually born into old money; his family has been rich for centuries. There is no way I would have ever found myself poor. It was quite a challenge because of the family I came from. Before I got married to Emerson, I was a simple waitress. His family fought against the kind of love that we had. They wanted someone at least in his grade. I was too low for them. Emerson defied them and got married to me. They even disowned him for some years when we had our first child, and we lived from hand to mouth. It was after we had our first son that they finally called him back," Olivia tells me later that day, when the children are asleep from all the activity of the day.

"Wow," I say. I expected that she had been wealthy all her life.

"My first daughter, Sarah, is married to Paul Wright," Olivia says, and then she looks at me as though she is expecting me to realize something. I haven't figured it out yet. I'm still lost.

"My first grandson is Alexander Wright, who is the father of your children," she reveals, and the realization dawns on me. I'm so shocked that I can barely open my mouth; not a word comes out of it. Everything makes sense now. That is why Olivia seems so familiar. She reminded me of Alex the very first day I met her. That was why Alexander had the same aura as his grandmother.

"No, no, he's not the father of my children," I correct Olivia and shake my head. I don't want anything to do with Alexander; he already denies me and my children. Why does his grandmother feel like they are his?

"Stupid boy. Alexander is very rash sometimes, and I do not doubt that he actually said that. I already confirmed that these children are his, and you know this too. You might not want to admit it, but it is actually true. The children look so much like Alexander. Layla looks exactly like Anne did when she was a child," Olivia says, and I shake my head. Alexander's words to me come back in full force, and I feel tears sting my eyes. I cannot bear to be in that situation again.

"It doesn't matter if he is their biological father; he rejected us and insulted me. He made me feel like nothing. He left me alone to care for my children and never looked back. I cannot forgive him," I say. It is the truth; even after six years, I am still deeply hurt by what happened between me and Alex. I am sure that I will still be in pain for years to come.

"My grandson has clearly made some very costly mistakes, and I cannot apologize on his behalf. I know that he has hurt you; I just ask for a chance to know my great-grandchildren. I want my grandson to know his wrongs and do right by you. It's alright if you don't want to see him again after this, but just let him know that he has three children living somewhere. Let the children know that they have a father, even if he is a crappy one," Olivia says. I can hear the sense in what she is saying, but I'm still hurt, and it's hard for me to accept it. The memory of how he rejected me keeps coming back over and over again, fresh as the day he struck the blow.

"He will not believe that the children are his anyway; he will push us away like he did when I told him I was pregnant," I say.

"My grandson likes to be meticulous about these things, but he has also been hurt. I am not excusing him, but he will be looking for some form of proof, which I already have. He will be obligated to accept the children. They will have his name," Olivia says.

I don't need to prove anything to anyone. "If he wants to believe that the children are his, then he is free," I say, then stand up from the couch. I'm not in the mood for this discussions anymore. I just want to go back home. I knew that there would be drama when I came to California, but this was the last thing that I expected.

"Just think about it and make the best decision for you and the kids," Olivia says, but I'm barely listening to her. I'm also angry with her, because if she had told me all this on the phone, I would have never agreed to come to the States. She wants me to see her grandson, or at least she wants the children to see their father. I'm not sure what will be best for the children. My mind flies back to when they asked me about their dad and I had no answer to give them. In this case, I will be able to give them an answer. It will be easier to explain that we didn't live with each other than to explain that they didn't have a dad at all. I think I will need to ask someone for advice, but I know that calling Maya won't be very helpful. She just doesn't like the guy. I would call Leo, but he hates Alex even more than I do. That being said, the decision is one that I have to make on my own. I have to look at things from all angles, as I'm not the only one involved. I have to consider three other people; I have to put their interests first.

That night, I sleep alone, thinking about the best decision I can make that will be favorable to everyone around me.

"Good morning," I say to Olivia, who is sitting in the dining room drinking her coffee.

"How was your night, Julia?" Olivia replies. "Come, eat breakfast; if there's something else that you would like, let Sonia know. She will make it for you."

"Thank you. The food is amazing," I say.

"Sonia is a great cook; she has been with me for ages," Olivia says.

I smile and nod.

"I'll let the kids meet Alex." I had come to the decision and steeled myself for what was to follow. Knowing I was risking my own heart. But they deserved to know the truth.

"Wonderful," Olivia replies with a smile. "I want to invite Alex for dinner tonight," she tells me.

"Okay," I say, even if I don't feel okay at all. Okay is the last thing I feel. I want the ground to open and swallow me. I want to run as far as I can, but I do not feel okay.

My heart begins to pound fast and hard against my ribcage. I'm not sure I'm ready to meet with Alex. It has been six years, but I'm still not willing to see him just yet. He still affects me so much..

"Are you sure you're alright with it? We can wait a while, or I can just send him the results; he doesn't have to come here," Olivia says, and I shake my head. As much as I don't want to see him, I actually want him to see me. I want him to take back what he said and acknowledge that I was, in fact, telling the truth that day. I want him to see all the children and accept that he is their father. I'll be able to make it through seeing him even if it's only for that, and it will be more than worth it.

"He should come. I will like him to come to dinner," I say, and Olivia nods.

"I'll go get the kids ready," I say, and I get up from. It will be the first time they are meeting their dad, and while this is no fault of theirs or mine, it is best that they make an impression on him. They have been doing very well without him for years, and they don't need him for his money. I can support them all by myself. I need to get ready too. I haven't seen Alex in the past six years, and I need to show him that I'm not the pitiful twenty-one-year-old he met years ago.

I have grown into a beautiful and successful woman.

That afternoon, the kids and I go on an even deeper exploration of the mansion. It seems even larger on the inside than it is on the outside. The building has an entire ballroom for hosting parties and other events. There is a music room filled with instruments; the house appears to be more of a museum than a typical home.

As the day crawls closer to evening, I sit the kids down to prepare them for dinner.

"We are expecting a guest for dinner, so we all have to be on our best behavior," I tell my children, and they all nod.

"Who is coming for dinner?" Luca asks, and I'm taken aback for a minute. I don't know what to say. Should I tell them that it is their father? What if he doesn't come? I don't know how I will deal with the aftermath.

"Just someone important; you will see him when he gets here," I say. They are all dressed, and so am I. I am wearing a simple, flowing red dress that stops at my knees. It is simple yet classy, and I think I'm looking really good. The children are also dressed simply, not like they were going out but staying home for dinner.

Olivia has the test results with her, and she says she will give them to Alex when he comes. I can't wait for him to read them and see his reaction. I know that just looking at the children and me will be enough for him, but the test will be there to seal the deal.

I'm nervous as I wait for Alex to arrive, partly because I got ready too early, and now I'm just waiting for it to be time for dinner.

"Oh, Alex, you're here," Olivia says, and I look toward the door. The children are watching a cartoon, but I can't bring myself to focus on anything. I hear Alex's voice, and my heart feels like it's going to fly out of my chest.

"Jocelyn," Olivia says, and I'm in shock for a moment. I didn't think that Alex would come with someone.

"Good evening, Olivia," the lady says. The fact that Alex's partner is female makes things more disconcerting. I never even stopped to think that maybe he would be in another relationship or that maybe he had moved on with his life and didn't want anything to do with me anymore. And that is what happened.

They all walk into the living room, and my breath hits the ground when I see Alex. His eyes met mine, and I can tell that he recognizes me the moment he sees me. It makes me feel good that he recognizes me after six years. I held his mind that much.

"Alexander, Jocelyn, this is Julia and her children, Landon, Layla, and Luca," Olivia says, and Alex looks at the children for the first time; the shock on his face is so obvious, he actually staggers a bit. He can see the resemblance. I let out a breath that I didn't know I was holding. I wanted him to believe me, at least subconsciously. I wanted him to accept that the children were his when he first met them, without the test.

"Grandma," Alex says, managing to open his mouth for the first time, and she shrugs.

"I didn't know you would bring Jocelyn," Olivia says.

"Am I missing something here?" the lady asks. She is quite cold; the aura that she exudes is like someone without emotions. She must be the woman Alex is with, yet she is so alike to him that I know that it won't work. It's not like I can control whom Alex wants to be with, but I know that this girl, Jocelyn, is not right for him.

"It's a family matter," Olivia says, and Jocelyn blinks in confusion.

"Uhmm, Jocelyn. Can you take the car and go home? Please, we can have dinner another time. I need to deal with this," Alex tells her. She looks around and at the children like she's about to complain, but she nods her head.

After Jocelyn is gone, Olivia smiles at her grandson.

"Okay, Alex, let's go and have dinner," she says, and Alex looks at me then, confused.

What's going on, Grandma? Do you know Julia? Who are those kids?

"If you insist, Alex. I invited Julia here for dinner. I met her when I was in the Bahamas a couple weeks ago. She went to the Bahamas for a wedding; she was there with the children. I could see the resemblance right away. How could you, Alex? Why did you not even investigate after she told you she was pregnant? Why did you just turn her away?" Olivia shouts at her grandson. I didn't even know she was that angry at Alex, and it shocks me to see her shouting at him.

Alex can't even say a word; he just looks at his grandmother, clearly ashamed.

"You can't deny them now. You have your proof!" Olivia shouts again and gives Alex the envelope. He takes it from her and opens it. I can't read the expression on his face when he reads it.

"Ah!" Olivia exclaims before she swoons, holding her chest. I run to her immediately, but Alex reaches her before I do.

"Nana Olivia!" the children shout and move toward her. They're scared for her. I can hear the fear in their voices. I'm afraid for her too.

"Olivia, are you okay?" I ask as we lay her down, but she looks so pale. She's still clutching at her chest.

Alex is already calling the doctor to attend to her immediately. The evening is taking an ugly turn, and we haven't even eaten yet. I sit by Olivia and hold her hand tight until the doctor comes. She looked so strong and healthy for the past few days that I actually believed that she wasn't sick, even when she told me herself that she had been sick previously.

I wouldn't be able to live with myself if something happened to her today when she was angry with her grandson because of me. I want Alex to accept his children, and know that I wasn't lying all those years ago, but not at the expense of Olivia.

The doctor finally arrives, and I leave Olivia as he attends to her.

I am in Olivia's room with Alex, the man that I have avoided for so many years, and I have no words to say.

I look at him and then back at my hands, and I just pray that Olivia is alright, above everything.

CHAPTER NINE

ALEX

I'm shocked when I see Julia up close for the first time in six years. The woman who tried to pin a pregnancy on me is the last person I thought I would see at my grandmother's place. Jocelyn and I had a dinner date planned before my grandma called to say she needed to see me urgently. I didn't want to stand Jocelyn up, because I always do that. Our relationship is barely there at this point, and if we have to get married, we should at least know each other. It was something that the two of us agreed on, but because we're both always working and business moguls are only interested in work, it's hard to draw us out, we barely have any free time together.

I figured that Jocelyn and I could have a nice date with my grandma before we went out again later. One can imagine how shocked I was to see Julia there in my grandmother's living room. There are times that I think back to how I handled the situation, and guilt overpowers me. I try to convince myself that she was lying and that there was no way that she was pregnant with my child. Even when I had her tracked and realized that she was actually pregnant, I told myself that the child wasn't mine because I'd used a condom. Yet she is here now with my grandmother and three children who look just like me after more than six years.

I look at my grandma as she introduces her and her children. I barely noticed them before now. There are three of them, and once I see them clearly, it feels like my heart hits my stomach. I feel so sick, I almost close my eyes out of regret. The children are clearly mine. There is no way I can deny it, even if I wanted to, and I don't want to. I just feel so bad for not believing her when she told me the truth. I left the woman with three children to take care of on her own. From what I knew, she was a student at the time. Things just got worse and worse.

I even forget that Jocelyn is standing there; she doesn't seem to have made the connection yet, but I know that she doesn't need to be here for this. I tell her to take my car and go home. I apologize, and while she is clearly confused, she does leave, and I am grateful.

As soon as she's gone, my grandma unleashes her anger on me. She tells me how she met Julia and how disappointed she is in me. She gives me the DNA test that proves that the children are mine, and I can't even start processing the fact that I am a father. I can't blame my grandmother for her anger. I deserve it, and some might say I deserve more. I won't even argue. I was incredibly terrible for leaving those children without a father; my only excuse is how Genevieve treated me. I began to think only of the worst of women.

I am still deep in my thoughts when my grandmother holds her chest and lets out a strangled cry. I move to hold her, and Julia rushes to her. I felt immensely guilty immediately. Things are quickly taking a worse turn. The children are crying for their Nana, and I call the doctor immediately. I will not be able to live with myself if something happens to my grandmother now because she was shouting at me for being irresponsible, which isn't a lie. Before the doctor arrives, Julia does all she can to bring my grandmother comfort; she clearly has some kind of relationship with her. She cares for her. The children are standing at the far corner with me because their mother said Nana wants to rest.

I can't bring myself to really look at them because I keep seeing myself in all of them. There is a bit of Julia in the girl, but she is basically a female me; she looks so much like Anne, my twin sister. Anne has a son of her own, and my grandmother has been itching for other great-grandchildren for so long. I would never have expected that she already had three somewhere in the world. The children are talking with each other, and I notice that they have a bit of an accent—an Australian accent. That's where she has been for the past five years.

I want to talk to them, but I don't know what I will say. I'm still struggling with the reality that I'm the father of six-year-old triplets. It seems too big and too much for me to imagine. I remove my mind from all of that as the doctor comes in; my grandmother needs to be fine. I want to call my mother, but I don't want to worry her, either. Maybe when the doctor has cleared her. Julia moves away from the doctor and comes to me while we both watch him work.

The air is so tense that a knife can cut through it. We don't say anything to each other for a while. We just stare at each other.

"I'm sorry," I say to her. The words aren't enough; words will never be enough, but I say them. They seem like all I can do. I can't turn back time to change my actions or retrace my steps so that I don't make any mistakes. With her body language and her expression, I can tell that she is angry and that my apology isn't what she wants to hear, but I must at least say the words.

"Your grandmother just suffered some shock, but she is okay now. I prescribed some drugs for her, and I will advise that she come to the hospital to run a few tests tomorrow," the doctor says before he leaves, and I breathe a sigh of relief.

"She just needs some rest; she can eat and then retire for the day," he continues, and I nod.

"Thank you, Doctor," I say, and Julia thanks him too before he leaves.

She leaves me standing in the room, and the children go with her.

"Julia, wait!" I say as she is leaving, I need to talk to her. I need to have at least a few words with her. I need to explain why I was like that with her. She stops, and turns back to me. She doesn't look happy with me at all; she looks vexed and annoyed.

"What is it?" she asks. Her voice sounds so cold, and I think of all that she had to endure on her own, and I know that whatever treatment she feels like giving me, I deserve it, and more. She has gone through all of that, and I just rejected her cruelly.

"I need to talk to you," I say, and she shakes her head.

"I want to inform the cook to make some soup for Olivia and then serve my children dinner so they can go to bed; I don't have the time to talk to you, or anyone at all," she says, and then turns on her heel. I'm rooted to the spot for a while, and I sigh. She will need time, and I also need time to analyze my situation and find out what I need to do. There is still Jocelyn. Oh God, what do I do with her?

The only reason I agreed to the contract marriage that will bring Jocelyn's company and me together was because I knew that love wasn't something she was interested in and that would be the only way I would get married. Women, as I thought, were traitors, and there were very few who were not. The rare gems were reserved for the best of men, and I was not among them. My mother had been pressuring me to get married, and so I'd agreed to marry Jocelyn without knowing that I had three children. Jocelyn and I are not wed yet, but we are engaged, and the wedding is in two months. The children changes everything. I know that Jocelyn will not agree to be married if she knows that I have other children. The major reason she had agreed at all was because she wanted more power. I didn't find anything wrong with her terms for marriage previously, but now things can't be the way we planned them.

In just one day, my entire life was turned upside down.

Oh, God, I need a drink.

I sit down in my grandmother's living room and close my eyes. I have a feeling that my life is going to become a whirlwind.

***

JULIA

I feel like breaking down. The load I'm carrying is far too heavy, and I need to drop it; if not, I will faint. My children seem to notice my mood and are unnaturally calm during dinner. Alex is still in the house; I know this, but I don't look for him. I just fed my children and got them ready for bed.

"Is Nana Olivia dead?" Luca asks as I'm tucking him in, and I'm shocked and almost fall. I shake my head vigorously.

"Oh no, she's not dead; she's just sleeping," I say to them, but the triplets don't seem convinced by my words. "She's not feeling too well; that's why the doctor came to see her. He says she should rest. By tomorrow morning, Nana Olivia will be all right," I explain. It's easy to reassure them because they know the truth.

"I thought she was dead, just like our Daddy," Layla says. I didn't know that I could receive that much shock in one day, but I feel it.

"Who is filling your heads with all of this? Your dad isn't dead, Layla, and neither is Nana Olivia," I say to the children. I'm so dumbfounded by the fact that they feel their father is dead. But then again, that is what many people assumed since they are growing up without a father; the man must be dead.

"Then where is he?" Landon asks. It takes me a while to understand his meaning. "If Daddy isn't dead, then where is he?" Landon asks again. I feel like screaming for Alex. I feel like shouting that he should explain himself to his children and let them know that they have a father who is not six feet under, but so much has happened today that I don't think they are ready for that information yet.

"Your father is fine, and you will see him very soon, okay? Let's go to sleep now." I try to convince them.

"Is he the man that was in the living room then? That was what Nana Olivia said; that was why she was screaming and shouting so loud," Luca says, and I close my eyes in frustration. I had no idea that they were listening while Olivia was talking to Alex. I even forgot they were in the room entirely. I shouldn't have let them be there.

"I will let you meet your father tomorrow. But please, no more questions; Mommy is tired," I tell my children. They seem to listen to me, finally, and they go to sleep.

I know that tomorrow morning, I will not even wake up before they drag me off to show them their father. I have to talk to Alex before that happens.

When did things get this bad?

I walk out of the children's room and consider where to go next. I want to go to my room and sleep because it has been a long day, but I still have to talk to Alex to let him know about the new development and to ask him about his plans concerning the children. But then again, I don't want to talk to him first; I want to get the opinion of someone else. He apologized to me, but an apology is not what I need. Olivia is still sick, and I need to check on her before I finally go to bed.

I should call Maya; she's the best person to talk to at this point. I walk to my room and bring out my phone to call her, and even though it's late, she still picks up my call.

"Hello, Maya. I'm so sorry to disturb you. I'm having a bit of an issue right now, and I need your advice," I say to my friend, and I proceed to tell her all that has occurred in the past few days.

"What are the odds? This seems like something out of a movie script," Maya says, and I agree with her that it does seem surreal. If someone had told me this, I would have thought they were making it up, but it was happening to me in real life.

"So, what do you think I should do?" I ask her, and she breathes deeply.

"This is tricky. Considering how much of a bastard he is and how much you have suffered over the years, all alone, I'd say you should let him stew and let him beg to be the father of your children. He doesn't deserve it at all, but you still have to think of Olivia; she at least deserves her great-grandchildren. Your children do need a father; it doesn't have to be their biological father, but since he knows and is willing to take care of them, you should let him. Ask him for his plans and what he wants, and then tell him what you want and let him know your wants are what will go. "But don't let your hurt deprive your children of a father," Maya says, and I smile. It's easier said than done because I'm not even sure I can talk to Alex without bursting into tears or trying to maim him because of how angry I am.

"I will try my best to be balanced and not let my children miss a father," I say to Maya before I disconnect the call. I have to talk to Alex the next morning if I can't tonight.

I go to Olivia's room and see that she is fast asleep. I've begun to look at this woman like my own grandmother. I loved her so much, and it broke me when she died.

"I already told my mom and dad what happened; they will be here tomorrow to see her," Alex says. I didn't even know he was there, and turn to face him, shocked. I look at him, and instantly want to flee. I'm not interested in having a conversation with him, but then again, I know that I must. He is the father of our children, whether or not I like it.

"The children are asking about you," I say, and I don't elaborate. He looks confused, but then realization dawns on him, and he nods.

"I want to tell them that you are their father and that they have one," I continue. He doesn't seem to have any problem with this, as he nods again.

"What are their names?" he asks, and I am lost, as the question is random. "I wasn't really listening when my grandmother introduced them for the first time," he clarifies.

"Oh, the firstborn is Landon; he is very active, so it's quite obvious who he is, even if he is identical with the second born, Luca. Luca is more quiet and reserved. Layla is the third and the girl," I say, and he nods like he is actually interested; maybe he is, but it will be hard for me to forgive him for pretending as though the last six years didn't happen.

"The names are very nice. I'm still trying to grasp the fact that I have

71

three children, all mine. All in one day. I would like to meet them and introduce myself, if that is okay with you," Alex says, and I nod. I'm annoyed, though, because he's taking it all so simply, like nothing huge happened and just saying sorry can fix all the years that I spent alone, the insults that I faced, and the marginalization.

"Tomorrow, you can introduce yourself to the children, but that is it. They will know that you are their father, and you can act like a father to them, but that is where it ends. I don't want to be in a relationship," I say to him. I don't want anything to do with Alex, and I feel it is best that I let him know at this moment instead of waiting and then bringing it up later or Alex being angry because he expected something from me. Alex looks like he wants to argue or say something, but he nods.

"Thank you; I will talk to the children tomorrow, and we will probably plan a dinner to introduce them to the rest of the family," he says. The fact that there is still family to meet is the one thing I love most about this, because my children will be part of a big family.

"I'm okay with that," I say. I'm surprised by how easy it is to talk to him; maybe I was overthinking after all. I want to ask him how his fiancée will react to the children, but I figure that is none of my business.

"I noticed that the children have a bit of an accent; you have been living in Australia?" Alex asks, and I nod. I don't want to go into the story of how and why I chose to live there. That is too much for me.

"Yes, I have been there for the past five years," I say, and Alex nods.

"You have a job over there?" Alex asks, and I shrug.

"I'm a software engineer; I can work anywhere," I simply say, "I want to brag about all that I have achieved over the years, but I know that will even be too much for me. I want to let him know that I have come so far and that I can do anything without him. I am very proud of all I have been able to achieve over the years, and I know that my circumstances pushed me to be the best.

"That is very nice. I don't mean to sound crass, but I'm impressed. Three children is a lot, and yet you were able to care for them and hold a job; it just makes me feel more and more like a bastard," Alex says, and I smile. He is a bastard, and I feel good that he is feeling remorseful at the very least.

"I have a live-in nanny; Ariana didn't come with me for this trip, but the triplets are more than a handful; I doubt I could have done it alone," I say, and then I stop myself as I realize that I'm talking to Alex too freely. I'm too happy with him. I'm supposed to hate him because he hurt me so deeply.

"I'm exhausted; if you will excuse me, I would like to take my rest," I say, and then I walk out on him and go to my room.

That night, when I close my eyes , I pray that the next day will not be as tumultuous as this one.

CHAPTER TEN

JULIA

"Mommy, can we meet Daddy yet?" Layla is the first one of the children to ask, and while Landon is the boldest of all my children, Layla is the one who is most concerned about the daddy issue. I know that the fact that she is a girl plays a role in that, and I am actually grateful that I can now show the children their father.

"He will be here very soon," I say, and I put more pancakes on her plate. We are all having breakfast, including Olivia. She woke up earlier than everyone else that morning and went for her morning jog. She claimed that she was just a bit out of sorts yesterday and that she is fine now.

Alex looked at her then like she was crazy, but he couldn't do anything to her. Olivia isn't surprised by the children's questions that morning; she seems quite pleased with herself, even knowing that she has great-grandchildren. I can't help but be happy for her. She is at least fulfilled.

As though he knew the children were talking about him, Alex walks in with a smile.

The children also seem to know something that I don't, as they smile when they see him. They then look at me as though sharing a message. I want to say it's not him, but Alex is their father, so I ignore them and focus on my food.

"Julia," Alex says as he sits down. I raise my head and give him a tight smile. I don't want to let down my guard around him; I don't trust him.

"Alex," I say and nod at him. He also greets his mother, and we all eat together. The children seem to be rushing their meals, and they finish before even I finish mine.

"We're done, Mommy," Layla says smartly, and I nod. I clear my throat and look at Alex. He realizes that I'm signaling him, and he smiles and drops his fork.

"Let's go to the living room, children," I say, and the kids stand up with me. They're so excited to know their father that I can ask them to do anything and they would agree, no questions asked.

"Good morning, Landon, Luca, and Layla," Alex says to the children. They look so enthusiastic to be listening to him. It's almost like they already know what he wants to say. They already knew that he is their father.

"Good morning," they chorus back.

"Uhmm, my name is Alex, and I'm your dad," he says awkwardly. The children will make wonderful actors, as they all show obviously fake shocked expressions. I almost laugh when I see them, but then I remember how serious the situation is, and I frown. I shouldn't be laughing about anything that concerns Alex, so I calm myself.

"Oh really?" Layla asks dramatically. It's almost like they want Alex to know that they were previously aware of the fact.

"Yes," Alex says, nodding his head. He looks to me for some help, but I ignore him.

"Where have you been?" Luca asks. He sounds serious, but Luca always sounds serious; that's simply him. My second son tends to ask questions that a normal six-year-old would not ask.

"I have been around, but I did something very bad. But from now on, I am your Daddy, and I will not leave you," Alex says, and I almost tear up—well, until I shake the feeling off. He's supposed to do all this, and more.

Luca seems satisfied by Alex's reply, and he nods.

"So, we can call you Daddy now?" Landon asks. My usually talkative son is quiet when it comes to Alex. I wonder if there's something else to this. I'll try to talk to them later and figure out how they feel about their father.

Yes, you can. I'd like that a lot," Alex says. Even though I'm angry at him, I have to cut him some slack. If he believed that the children were his, he would have taken care of them from the start. Because now, just a few hours after finding out about the children, he is so open to them. They seem to like him very much.

"Can we ask you for stuff, too?" Layla asks, and I raise an eyebrow at my daughter.

"Yes, you can ask me anything," Alex says, and I wonder what my daughter wants to ask her father for. I give them everything that they need and almost everything that they ask for. Of course, there are things that I cannot get, like unicorns or something, but I care for them well enough, and I don't want

Alex to think otherwise.

My daughter doesn't seem to share my line of thinking, though, as her words shock me.

"Daddy, can I have a hug?" Layla asks, and Alex looks like he's about to cry. He is clearly confused at first, and I think I have to help him. This is so emotional, even for me, and Layla didn't ask to hug me.

"Of course, come here, pumpkin," Alex says, and Layla skitters over to him. He bends down to hug her tight, and he holds her for a while. I feel like crying then. Olivia comes and watches them too.

"He found his way pretty early," Olivia says, and I nod. I can see that he will love them well. At least I don't have to worry about the quality of love that he will give to our children. I sigh a bit; the triplets are no longer just my children; I now share them with someone. I find that I like that feeling a lot.

"Come here, boys," Alex says, and the boys stand up from the chair immediately. With no hesitation, they run to their father, and he hugs all of them together. I feel so good to be part of their family. They look so beautiful together. I remind myself that he hurt me and that he is getting married to someone else; we cannot be family. And very soon, I will go back to Australia with the children, and the only communication they will have will be by phone and on holidays. I don't want to be without my children, so their visits will probably be short. I'm already planning and bending my life for a man who left me while I was pregnant. I have to forgive him, though; I still have to think of my children. It's just so painful.

Alexander's family home is a lot less extravagant than Olivia's place. It's pretty small and homey. The triplets and I are here for dinner and their introduction to his world. I'm nervous about how the rest of the family will take the news. I know that many people will read it differently. And I don't want a scene at all, but Olivia is here, and I know that she will fight for me.

Sarah, Alex's mother and Olivia's first daughter, is her carbon copy, except that she is calm in her aura and doesn't exude the aura of power that Olivia does. Her husband Paul is calm as well. Alex seems to have skipped his parents' energy and gone straight to his grandmother's.

Alexander's twin sister, Anne, is who Layla took after. It's very obvious when I first see her. My daughter just took my eyes, and that was it. Layla looks more like a lady that I had never met than she does me.

Anne arrives with her husband Richard and their daughter Kiara who is five years old. She sits down close to the triplets and the resemblance between Kiara and Layla is so uncanny that I'm sure that no one in the room misses it.

Cooper, Alex's younger brother, is also here. Jocelyn, the cold lady I met the other day, is here too. The table is full. Everyone is looking at the children, and I see surprise in their eyes. I know that even before I say anything, it's obvious who we are and why we are at the house.

Dinner is long, and I'm nervous the entire time. The children seem to be having a great time, though, meeting their new cousin, even though they haven't been introduced. I can see that they all know it.

"I have an announcement to make," Alex says after dinner is over and all eyes turn to him. I know that everyone knows, but he still has to say it.

"Uhhm, the triplets, Landon, Luca, and Layla, are my children," Alex says, and conversations start to buzz all around.

"Congratulations, Alex," Anne says, standing up to hug her brother.

"I have so many questions," Cooper says with a laugh. I smile at that, too. I would be confused if my family just arrived with three six-year-olds and told me they were a part of it.

"Uhmm, Julia told me that she was pregnant, but I assumed that the child could not be mine. She was clearly angry with me and went on to raise the children on her own. Grandma met her in the Bahamas and knew immediately that they were my kids. I'm going to take responsibility for them now," Alex says uncomfortably.

"That is good, son," Paul says. I look around, and I realize that everyone looks happy, except Jocelyn. I don't blame the lady; she's probably thinking of what it would mean for her. If I were in her shoes, I would have the same thoughts.

"What do you mean take responsibility?" Jocelyn asks, and it's almost like she has been holding herself back and can no longer resist blurting out questions, so she bursts out with shouting.

Alex looks at her as though he can't believe that she's asking such a question.

"I mean, I will give them my name, and I will take care of my children.

I'll give them everything they're supposed to have," Alex says, and I can't help but smile at that. Jocelyn doesn't seem to share the same sentiments with me, as she looks furious at what Alex said.

"Can't you just pay off the bitch and the children or something? Do you actually have to take care of them? They just came out of nowhere. For God's sake, we have a contract, and you can't just break it off. We're getting married in a month. If you decide to keep these children, then the contract is over!" Jocelyn says. She refers to my children in such a vile manner that I stand up to tell her exactly what I think of her. But Jocelyn walks out of the dining room before anyone can say anything to her.

"She is crazy!" Cooper says. I think I will like Alex's younger brother very much. I'm still pissed at what Jocelyn said, and I'm angry that I didn't have the chance to respond. I sit down in my chair, albeit reluctantly.

"I'm sorry, Julia," Alex says, but I don't reply. While this isn't his fault, all he does is apologize. It annoys the hell out of me.

"Jocelyn is just annoyed that things aren't going the way she wants them to. I'll talk to her. I knew as soon as she met the children that our marriage wouldn't work out; she won't marry me knowing I have other children. She wants her children to have power, and if I have other children, it defeats the purpose," Alex says later when he's driving me home, and I nod.

"Did you love her?" I ask. I don't want him to lose the woman that he loves because of the children. I'm relieved for more than one reason when he shakes his head.

"It was just going to be a contract marriage," he says, and I nod.

"Will it hurt your business too much to leave her?" I ask, and he shrugs.

"There are losses and there are gains. Besides, the children are worth it a thousand times over," he says, and I smile. I love that he loves them.

"The children are excited to have a new family; they have more possibilities for cousins," I say. "I'm the only child of only children. I wanted many children, and it was a blessing that I had triplets, but it didn't come the way I expected it to."

"Yes, my family is a big one; you haven't met my mom's siblings yet. Grandma's other children, my father's siblings—we all come together for Christmas," Alex says, and I smile. I can imagine how full the mansion would be during Christmas. Maybe that's why she has such a big house.

"It's the only time that my grandmother's house doesn't feel empty. I don't know how she lives there when it's not Christmas. You're comfortable there, aren't you?" Alex asks, and I nod.

"Yes, the children and I are very comfortable; they think the house is a castle. It seems like a castle to me, too," I say with a smile. We reach Olivia's house, and the children and I get out and wave him goodbye.

"I'll come over tomorrow, and we'll go out. I'll take you all to the amusement park my dad took me and my siblings to as children," Alex says, and the children cheer. They want to see the amusement park. I want to see the park too, I realize. We all go inside, and I help them take their baths and tuck them all in bed. I reach for my phone and see that I have had ten missed calls, all from Leo. I frown when I see the missed calls. Is something wrong? Did something happen at home? I haven't talked to him since I left Australia more than a week ago, and I did say I would stay for just a weekend.

"Hello, Leo. How are you doing?" I ask when I call him back.

"I'm doing very well. I don't know about you. Did you decide to move to California and you didn't let me know?" Leo asks, and I laugh.

"Too much has happened, Leo. I have to be here just for a while yet," I say, and he sighs.

"I miss you and the kids a lot; you guys should come back home already," Leo complains, and I laugh out loud.

"You won't believe all that has happened since I've been here. Olivia is actually Alex's grandmother.

"Alex?"

"Yes, Alex. The same Alex that you know."

"I knew something was fishy. She wouldn't just ask you to come like that without a catch," Leo says, and I shake my head and then tell him in detail everything that had happened from the beginning up until now.

"So he broke up with his fiancée?" Leo asks.

"Yes."

"He's going to ask you to stay with him," he concludes.

"No, he has no right to do that. There's no way I will stay here; I have a life in Australia." Leo sighs like he doesn't believe me, and for the life of me, I can't understand why.

"It won't stop him from asking."

"I will say no." I don't have another answer; none seem plausible to me. I don't think that Alex will ask me to stay; nothing he has done so far has led me to believe that, so it might just be Leo talking.

"Do you think he will be a good father to the triplets?" Leo asks. I have to be truthful about this. From what I have seen, they would not have a better father.

"Yes, he will take good care of them; he already does," I say with conviction.

"Even if he is a bastard, he is a good father, and that's fair enough," Leo says, and I laugh. It's the name that I've used to refer to Alex all these years. Fucking bastard. I can at least testify to the fact that the bastard loves his children.

"Come home soon, Julia."

"I'll be back before you know it."

"We're going to the amusement park! Going to the amusement park! We're going to the amusement park!" the children chant as Alex drives to the park. They're so excited about this whole trip that one would think they never went to amusement parks in Australia.

"With Daddy!" Layla shouts, and Alex smiles. I know that he is the CEO of Wright's Corporation, and it hasn't occurred to me until now that he does so much for the children. His phone never rings when he is with us, and he is always available.

"Don't you have to be at work?" I ask him as the children are enjoying the merry-go-round at the huge amusement park.

"I took a vacation. It's been years since I had one," he says with a smile, and I nod. He's doing so much that I wonder yet again if he really is going to ask me to stay. I'm skeptical about his kindness after what Leo told me. I don't want him to ask me to stay, because I'm afraid that I will want to. I want to keep being angry at him, but it's so hard seeing how he is with the children; he clearly loves them, and this makes me want to love him too. I can't love him; I can't love a man who so easily left me.

"Okay," I say, and I ignore him as I look at my children; they're so excited as they scream and wave in the ride. We go to other rides, and Alex buys them cotton candy.

"I love you, Daddy; I want to be with you forever and ever," Layla says. I want to think that it is just the sugar talking and that she is just a child, but I'm beginning to feel that it will be very hard to separate these children from their father and they won't want to go back home. That they won't see Australia as home anymore.

"I love you too, pumpkin," Alex says. The boys rally around him as he takes them on yet another ride. They all play the ring games, and Alex wins Layla a gigantic teddy bear. I don't think my daughter will be able to carry the thing, but she proves me wrong and holds it tight. We all get ice cream together, and at the end of the day, we're all exhausted, and it's time to go back home.

Daddy, will you stay with us today? at Grandma Olivia's house?" Layla asks her father as he drives us home, and I feel another pang in my chest She won't be able to say goodbye to Alex.

"Of course. I will stay behind and tuck you all in so that all the monsters go away," Alex says, and they all laugh. When I first met Alex, and even years later, I would have never imagined that he would be good with children, but he surprised me. He is very talented with them.

"Daddy, Daddy, can we come to your house?" Landon asks this time. My first son has opened up to his father completely. They all love him at this point.

"Of course, if your mom says it's okay, then we can go tomorrow," Alex says, and all the children look at me with pleading eyes.

"Please, Mommy," Luca pleads, and I cannot say no to Luca.

"Okay."

"Yay!" they all shout.

I keep thinking about what will happen when it is time for me to leave.

CHAPTER ELEVEN

JULIA

For the past two weeks, Alex has changed in my mind from the bastard who left me to a doting father. The children have started attending their classes at school online, and it is becoming so hard for me to take my things and leave. Olivia's house is becoming even more than a home to me, and to be honest, I'm not sure if I like this development or not.

I want to be angry with Alex; I want the hurt that I feel to be justified, yet he doesn't do anything at all that warrants it these days. It's almost like the anger is my fault, and so I should simply stop being angry.

Leo's words keep coming back to me, yet I can barely keep hold of the feelings I'm starting to develop for the man who dropped me without a second thought.

The children went out with Alex the day on a little father-and-child date, and I am alone working on my job, yet I can barely do anything. This is expected, though. My mind goes back to my children, but this time it's not for their care. I'm not afraid that something will happen to them. I know for a fact that Alex will take good care of them and that they will be safe. My fear is a different one: a fear that they will fall too in love with their father and I will be pushed to the sidelines. Or worse, I will be pushed to join them.

The fire that I felt on the first day I met Alex is coming back, but I don't want it to. It was that fire that made it hurt so much when Alex pushed me away.

I refused to go with them today because I didn't want to get too close to Alex, and now I regret it because I don't want my children to get too close to him either. I don't want them to leave me behind.

"Julia." I hear my name from a familiar voice, and I look up from my laptop. It's Alex. I stand up and search for the children but don't see them.

"They're with their Nana," he says, and I nod. That is another thing that's hard for me to deal with. My children only had me before, and now they have a whole new family; they're barely in my sight. I'm not afraid of the attention they're receiving; it's just that I'm scared of how hard it will be for them to let go when it is finally time.

"Oh, okay," I say and nod. Alex is dressed in a simple white polo shirt, jeans, and sneakers. I imagined him to be someone who lived in suits previously, but now that image has been severed completely. He still looks oddly like me, in casual clothes, though.

"I missed your company today," he says simply, moving closer to me. I raise an eyebrow at his comment and his movement toward me.

"You wanted to see the children; you said so. I don't have to go with you all the time," I say.

"What if I want you to?" he asks, and I'm actually surprised by the question. I'm tongue-tied for the moment and can't answer him. He wants me to be with him. At first, there is a fluttery feeling, a nice and satisfied feeling, and I want to be with him too. But then the image of Alex telling me that I'm lying to him about the children comes to me. I curse myself for feeling good about his stupid offer. Anger replaces that sweet feeling. For someone who hurt me, he sure has a lot of nerve.

"What if you want me to?" I ask, and he nods and moves even closer to me. He tries to take my hand, but I don't want him to touch me. I just stare at his outstretched hands.

"Julia, I want you to be more than just the mother of my children," he says. He looks like he's searching my eyes for something, but I shake my head. I'm so angry at his audacity and insistence, that I feel like I might just burst into tears.

"You didn't even want me to be the mother of your children six years ago. Up until one month ago, you didn't care if I was alive or not! And now you want me to be more than the mother of your children?" I shout. I can barely hold myself back. I'm so pained about how everything has happened.

Alex closes his eyes at my words and cleans his face with his palms.

"Julia. I am sorry; I said I was. I don't have any excuses; I can't even give them. I was a cad, and I am still one. But it was six years ago. Do you not think you can forgive me?" he asks, and I shake my head immediately. I don't even have to think about that answer before I give a reply.

"No. I do not think I can forgive you for that. I think about all the pain that I faced as a result of those words. I think about how bad it would have actually been if not for Maya, who was by my side. I think of how bad it still is and how it seems I cannot find love if I have three children from another man. How do people assume that I am okay with so many things? It doesn't really matter to them that they are three children who were born on the same day. It doesn't matter that I may have just had a fling for one night. Many people did exactly what I did; they did even more, yet things like that didn't happen to them."

"Even for the children?" he asks, and I don't understand his meaning.

"I want to marry you, Julia. It might be too much for me to say this, but I want to get married to you for the sake of our children. I want them to have a complete family. I know that this is sudden, but I want you to know that this is my plan," he says, and I shake my head. I don't agree with this at all.

"What? Why do you care about a family unit now and not when you were turning me away? Did you not stop to think that maybe this girl was telling the truth? I don't have to stand here and listen to you spout nonsense," I say and walk out on him.

"Will you hold that day over me forever? Can we not just try to have a simple conversation without rehashing the past? Can we not even talk about the first day we met?" Alex asks, and I stop and turn back to him.

"No, we can't do that. I can never forget that day for the rest of my life. I was simply a college student before that day. I was a girl who was trying to move on in life. After that day, I became a depressed pregnant woman. There are several things that could have happened to me. There were days when life wasn't worth living. I didn't think I would survive bringing three children into the world at once. You know, before birth, they said my canal was too small, and I was told to have sex so that I could deliver. I couldn't do that, even if I wanted to; I was afraid of men. I felt like every single man was just like you and they would all hurt me in the end. I am broken because of that day, so we cannot stop talking about that day!" I am already crying, and the tears are rushing down my face. Alex tries to move closer to me, but I run away from him. I run until I get to my room, and I close my eyes and cry. I fall to the floor almost immediately, and the tears come hard and fast. I can't stop crying. I'm in so much pain that I can't hold it back. It almost feels like I'm crying the tears of so many years all at once, that I'm feeling the pain that I felt all these years because Alex ripped open the wound that I was trying to cover and that had been healing. I feel like the pain is going to overwhelm me.

I cry until I finally fall asleep from the tears.

When I wake up, it is late at night, and the first thing that comes to mind are the children. I want to search for them, but then I know that they are fine, and I'm just the one who is worrying. The children are probably with their father or grandmother. The second thing that I think of is what I will do. I cannot marry Alex; I can't stay with him, not even for my children. There is no reason why I should stay here anymore. It's better that I go back home. Right away, I start to pack my things.

I book a flight, and the best that I can get is for the day after tomorrow. So, the children can stay for one more day. They will be happy to spend it with their father. I will try my best not to separate them from him, but I know that it won't be easy for me at all. I know that at some point I will be the bad parent, but I'm willing to risk that.

When I'm done packing my things, I go to the children's room and begin to pack their things, too. They are all asleep. Over the next hour, I pack all the clothes and get ready for the next day. I see that they have so much more luggage than they came with. They have been here for so long that their luggage has doubled.

"I heard you had an argument with Alex today." I'm startled because I didn't expect anyone to come in so late at night. I turn back and sigh as I see Olivia.

"Who said so?" I ask dumbly. She chuckles lightly.

"I literally heard the argument, and I understand why you want to leave. You could use the space, and the children should be with you," Olivia says, and I sigh. It's not a simple decision, but I do not know how I want to tell Olivia that.

"I don't think I'm going to come back here," I say truthfully. It will be too hurtful to be so close to Alex.

"Not even for Christmas?" Olivia asks, and I'm shocked. I expect that she will ask if I won't let her great-grandchildren see her, and I was going to say that the children can come alone, but she is still on me.

"The children can come for Christmas," I say lightly. Christmas between the children and me was sweet and small, and it was just the four of us. Leo joined us last year, but he usually traveled home for the holidays.

"And you will spend Christmas alone?" Olivia asks, and oddly, I feel offended at this. I know that it is the truth, but I do not want to hear it.

"Maybe I will be with someone before Christmas," I say, and she raises an eyebrow at me.

"Maybe."

"I will miss you, dear girl," Olivia says, and I can't hold myself back; I stand up and hug her tight.

"Will you be okay?" I ask her. I know that she has grown attached to the children over the past month, and I also know that she is sick, but she doesn't like to worry her family about it.

"I'll be fine; I'm strong as an ox. I think I have about fifty more years in me," Olivia jokes, and I smile.

"Thank you so much for bringing me here. Even if I am a little hurt by the outcome of today, I am happy that the children came here and met their father. I'm glad that Alex was here and agreed to be the father of my children. I'm happy that they had a few moments together. If not for you, I would still be wondering what to tell my children the next time they asked about their father," I say to Olivia, and she smiles.

"You're welcome. These are things that we have to do for our family. I am grateful that I got to meet my great-grandchildren. The sickness in my heart has gone down for the moment; I am happy with them," Olivia says, and I hug her even more and hold her tightly.

Olivia stays with me, and in silence, we pack the rest of the children's clothes. By the time we are done packing, it is already morning.

The children are so excited that morning because, apparently, their father promised to take them to where he works. He's going to take the children to the company.

"Kiara says she has been there before and that the place is huge and lots of people are in it," Landon says; he is referring to his cousin now. I do not have the mental capacity to tell my son that there is a possibility that Alex may not come today. I know that he will be angry about what happened last night, and I don't really care about his anger, just how it will affect my children. I don't want them to be hurt because of him.

"I am sure that it is really big," I say. I knew Wright Corporation when I was a student here, but I had never been there. I just knew that it was a big company; it wasn't the kind of place that I just randomly went to.

"Kiara says that Daddy is the boss there, and everyone listens to him," Layla says proudly. I know that he is the CEO and that he started the company by himself years ago. He's the kind of man that women would consider a catch. It's odd that he'd want a contract marriage; a man like him can get any type of woman he wants. He doesn't even have to pay; just his handsomeness and his influence will do the job.

"Enough about all that; let's eat our breakfast," I say, and the children return to their food. When Alex walks in, I realize that I've been waiting for him. I want my children to at least have their last day with him. I haven't told them yet that we are going back home. I want to tell Alex first, and I know that they will resist, but I want him to back me up so that the children are not so sad.

"Good morning, Alex," I say, and he looks at me so intently, I wonder if my eyes are swollen and if it's obvious that I've been crying all night.

"Julia," he says before he looks at the children. It's almost like he's calling them, as they jump from their seats immediately and run to him.

"Pumpkin," Alex says, kissing Layla's hair. She leans in to kiss him and doesn't want to let go of his neck. At this particular point in time, a certain memory comes to mind. I can still vividly recall being on my father's knees when I was five years old and just hugging him tightly. My parents passed away before I turned six years old, so I only have a few memories of them, but I made sure to savor those memories and store them away in my heart. I will always cherish them.

"Landon and Luca," he continues, and then hugs the boys too.

"Alex, we're going back to Australia tomorrow," I say to him then, across the table. My children look to me immediately. They have identical shocked expressions on their faces.

Alex is more composed. It's almost like he expected me to do this after yesterday.

"Oh okay. It has been a while since you guys came here; you have to go home eventually," Alex says, and I'm a little pissed that he doesn't even try to make me stay.

"But, Daddy, we don't want to go home!" Layla whines.

"We want to stay here with you, Daddy." This time it is Landon.

"Mommy, please let us stay," Luca begs, looking at me. My son, to whom I cannot say no, is asking me to stay, but I have to say no this time. He has to understand I cannot stay here anymore; I am only hurting myself. I do not want to hurt my children, but I also have to think of myself.

"Your mommy has to go back home; she has things to do there, and you all have to go back to school. You all shouldn't worry, okay? You will see Daddy very soon. I will be with you before you know it," Alex says, but Layla is already crying.

I regret telling Alex we were leaving right now. I'm not even sure they will agree to go to the office and spend their last day together before we go back to Australia. They're getting so attached to him that I'm feeling a little left out.

"I want to see Daddy every day," Layla says, and Alex goes to pick her up.

"There are times, sweetheart, that we don't always get what we want. You will see Daddy, but not every day; maybe once a month. Daddy will fly to Australia, and we will have some time together," he tells Layla, who only holds him tighter.

"We should go to the office together and spend today with Daddy, okay, and then tomorrow Mommy and you guys will go back home," Alex says. Layla looks like she is about to burst into tears; Luca and Landon look the same, but they seem to understand what their father is saying; they all nod their heads.

"Okay, let's clean our faces and get ready to go."

I dress the children up in their prettiest practical clothes, and I go with them this time. I don't want to leave them alone with their father, and I also want the chance to see Wright's Corporation. The place is huge, and it scares me that the father of my children owns the entire building and pays the salary of the staff that works here.

For the rest of the day, we meet different people from the company who respect Alex well. We also meet some ladies who are obviously shocked to see the triplets. I even heard a couple of them talking about the kids when I went to use the bathroom. The staff generally love the children, and all in all, it's a good day.

Alex stays the night with the children; he even sleeps in their room. He wanted to be as close to them as he could be before they left. I don't blame him at all. If I loved someone and they were leaving, I would do the same.

CHAPTER TWELVE

JULIA

The children and I are back in Australia. The morning when we were supposed to leave was long and full of tears. Alex's parents, Paul and Sarah, came over to say goodbye to the children. It was really nice to see how they got so attached to them in such a short amount of time. I was quite surprised to see them at Olivia's house. Anne and Kiara also came along. The children were all in a hug for almost ten minutes; they didn't want to leave each other. I'm so grateful that I didn't book a morning flight, as I'm sure that we would have missed it.

Alex didn't talk to me throughout the entire day; he didn't try to tell me to come back or to stay. At the time when I made the decision to leave, I wasn't looking for someone to tell me to stay, but at the point of leaving, it occurred to me that I may not want to leave. I was still hurt, though. Watching everyone with tears in their eyes was touching. I've only known Olivia for a short period of time, but that lady holds a special place in my heart. I love her to death. I had to remind myself of the reason I was leaving. Alex had hurt me; I just couldn't accept his proposal to marry him just because of the kids. I need to think and figure things out, and I couldn't do that while I was there.

"You're mooning again," Leo says, and I sigh and look at him. The children have been sad since they came back home. I had to drag them to school, as they didn't have the stamina or the will to do anything at all. They remind me of when Alex walked away from me. I feel the same way, and that is the issue. I walked away from him this time; I did it willingly. Why do I feel so bad, then? Why do I feel all broken, like I did when he left me?

"I miss the States, I guess," I say truthfully. I miss Alex a lot. I have to remind myself that he is the one who hurt me and that I cannot forgive him. Once in a while, a little voice in my head will ask me. Why not? Why can't I forgive him?

"What really happened there? You came back one week ago, and it's been like you lost your treasure or something," Leo asks.

"I already told you; I left him. I didn't want to be there anymore. It was too painful for me," I say.

"You're behaving like it is painful for you to be here," Leo says, and I turn away from him. "I didn't think I would ever say this, but do you not think that you should forgive him? You're miserable without him," Leo says, and I look at him.

"That's not true. I don't want to forgive him, but I'm not miserable. I didn't tell you this, but he asked me to marry him; he said he wanted the children to have a complete family. Can you believe his nerve? To think that I'd actually marry him?" I ask. I'm already angry, but I want to show Leo that Alex is not the reason I am this way.

"There are several reasons I miss the States; I miss Olivia, and my children have been down since they came here. So I can't really be full of joy since they are sad," I say. I feel a strong need to justify myself.

"He asked you to marry him?" Leo asks. I frown at him then. Is that all he heard me say?

"Can you imagine the nerve? To marry him? Why would I do that?" I ask with a frown. I obviously expect him to be on my side, but it's very obvious that he is not.

"I feel like I have somehow fueled the hatred that you have for this man," Leo says. "Did he ever tell you why he did that all those years ago?" he asks, and I'm confused. "Why did he deny the children?"

"I don't know. I never asked. He only said he was a cad and that he didn't have excuses, but that's not the point. The point is, he actually had the audacity to ask me to marry him!"

"I'm not trying to undermine all that you have been through, Julia, but what if he made a very costly mistake and he is trying now to correct his mistakes? Do you think that you can at least open your heart to try and forgive him for the horrible mistake he made?" he asks, and I'm quiet for a bit. I can't believe that he's actually asking me to try and forgive Alex. I've been so bent on not forgiving him that I haven't even considered the option of just letting it go. Could it be that easy?

"I don't know, Leo. The mistake was a massive one, and I let him see his children. I did well in that respect, didn't I?" I ask, and he nods.

"Yes, you have done well. And I'm not asking you to forgive him for him; I am asking you to forgive him for yourself. In this case, it's a very selfish act, and you're not happy, Julia. You aren't letting yourself be happy because you don't want to forgive someone. "That's not a very sensible thing to do," Leo says, and I have to think about it. "You should let go so that you can make decisions that holding on to the past will not affect," he says.

I want to shout and scream that I'm not holding on to the past and that I went through so much with the birth of the triplets and everything, but I'm quiet. I know that Leo is right.

"We will talk later," he says before he leaves me to my thoughts.

Later, I call Maya; I want to hear from her. Her words are similar to those of Leo's; she says I should give him another chance and that marriage is a way to form a complete family. Even if it shouldn't be the only reason and that love should factor in, I do love Alex. I didn't want to admit it to myself, but I actually do love him. But what do I do with this realization, with everything that happened?

+++

Alex

It's been one week since I saw Julia and our children, and my life has been hell in that period. It's almost like I didn't have a life before them. I just find out about them a month ago, and Julia, Layla, Landon, and Luca snuck into my heart, and they will not leave. They're here to stay. I tried to get back to my normal life, going to work and running the company like I used to, but nothing seemed the same anymore. It is like my life had been so dreadful and I had no idea, not until Julia snuck into it with the triplets in tow. There's no way I can settle for the kind of family that I initially planned to have. Life with Jocelyn seems incredibly dull and dreary now. A few days ago, she came to my home to sympathize with me, or at least that's the way she put it. She wanted to let me know that the offer to get married to her still stood now that my children were out of the way.

"My children will never be out of my way, Jocelyn. I still very much love them, and I am still responsible for them," I told her. She actually looked shocked and disappointed. The look on her face annoyed me; it was almost like she expected me to reply differently. She actually thought that I abandoned the children, and that is why they left. It made me think for more than a moment, if that was that the kind of man she thought I was? No wonder Julia ran as far as she could. I would do the same if I met a man like myself.

And what we once had, the contract, is over. "There's nothing between us anymore," I said to her. That was my attempt to become a better person after this. I want to become the kind of man that my children will be proud to call a father.

"Those rats are gone; there's nothing stopping us from being together anymore," she complained. I almost lost my temper in that moment. I looked at the woman that I was so close to getting married to, and I was glad for Julia, who made me dodge that bullet. Jocelyn wasn't someone who understood joy and happiness; all she cared about was money and power, as she felt they were the only important things in life.

"Leave!" I seethed at her; she looked shocked at my tone, but she left my home and my life. After that encounter, I was quite lost, and I'm still lost as to what I want to do. I know that I love my children; the time that I spent with them is testament enough. It was the best time of my life. I will forever be grateful to Julia for giving birth to them. I have so much respect for this woman who was able to raise three kids while she was in school. The fact that I miss them so much is not to be disputed. But what are my feelings for their mother? My mind goes back to when I first met Julia, dressed in her little black dress and nursing her drink in Club Essence. It was her innocence that drew me to her—the fact that she clearly didn't belong there. All I wanted to do was whisk her away, and I did just that. That night with her was different from anything that I had previously experienced, and in a good way. I left because I was scared that it would become more than I wanted.

I left her and tried my best to forget her, but it was almost impossible. The past few weeks with her and the children have been wonderful. Just thinking about the way she absentmindedly flips her air, her smile, the aura of innocence that she still carries, and the fact that she loves my children and that she carried them and took care of them makes me fall in love with her.

I love her. There is no other way about it; I want a family with her, one that is complete with my children.

But she hates me; she's angry with me because of what happened all those years ago, and truly, I can accept it. I was terrible to her. I made a mess of it the last time when I asked her to marry me. I just assumed that she would say yes and that she would put her children first; it didn't occur to me that the pain that I put her through was still very much present. I asked her to marry me because I didn't want her to go back to Australia. I wanted to keep her in the States. I enjoyed the time that we had together, and I just assumed that if I asked her, she would say yes. I thought she would be grateful to have a stable home for her children and would want to stay. But I just ended up hurting her. I didn't tell her why I did all that back then; I didn't tell her that I loved her and that I wanted her to be my wife, yet I wanted her to accept my proposal. I wouldn't even agree to that offer.

It's best that I leave her alone so she can live her life. I truly don't deserve to have her as my wife, and she might be right that I don't deserve to have the children either. I need to let her stay in Australia and live her life as she sees fit.

However, no matter how much I tell myself that I made the right decision, I still can't bring myself to let go. I wonder if it would have been better if I didn't know about the children at all; if my grandmother had never met them, maybe then I wouldn't have so much regret. But then again, if I were given the chance to choose, I would still choose them, knowing them, loving them, and being a family with them, even if it was a long-distance relationship. I expect their calls every day. The video calls are the highlights of my day, and simply hearing Julia's voice lifts my spirit.

"You can simply go to Australia, you know." I look up from my laptop, which I have been staring at for quite a while, and look at my twin sister Anne. I'm not even surprised that she's able to get into my house; Anne can do whatever she wants if she puts her mind to it. Most of the time she couldn't be bothered, but when she decides to bother herself, she's quite a force to be reckoned with.

"What are you doing here, Anne?" I ask as she deposits herself on my couch, already making herself comfortable. My question isn't complete. What are you doing here when I clearly said I don't want company? I told my parents and siblings that I wanted to be alone ever since Julia and the kids went back to Australia. The period has been hard for me, and the last thing that I need is company. I want to mourn the loss of my family alone.

"I'm here to tell you to get off your ass and go get your family," Anne says, and I raise an eyebrow at her; she tends to be raw when she's pissed.

"Thank you for your advice, but I'm fine right here," I say, and my sister glares at me. If looks could kill, I would be six feet under.

"What do you mean, fine? You're miserable!" she shouts, and I wince at the shrillness of her tone.

"Thank you for pointing that out."

"So, what are you going to do about that?" she asks, and I shrug.

"Nothing."

"Nothing?" She looks at me like I've gone absolutely crazy, and I'm not in the mood to clear up her doubts about my apparent sanity.

"Nothing."

"Why?" Anne shouts, and I wince again. She's not usually the shouting type; hell, my sister is as calm as they get, so all this is out of character for her. I don't say anything in response. I'm not sure how my sister will take my reply, and it's not something I'll say out loud.

"My daughter misses her cousins; Grandma Olivia misses her great-grandchildren. I miss Alex, who was a father. Our parents aren't happy with how much you have changed; it's clear that you're not happy, Alexander. Why do you not even want to try? Why don't you want to fight for your happiness? Why will you not push for what you truly want?" Anne asks, and she's almost crying now, so I know that I have to reply. I can't keep her without a response.

"Because I don't deserve her, Anne," I say quietly, almost as though I don't want her to hear me, but she does, and it's clear that she does; the look on her face says it all.

"Oh, Alex." She stands up from the chair and walks up to hug me tight. I let my twin hold me for a moment before letting go.

"I understand that it may feel like this sometimes, but you don't have to be discouraged. What you did was terrible; I can at least admit that, but you still have to make her understand, tell her everything, tell her about Genevieve and the baby, show her love, and do things for her. It will take some time, but I know you will be able to win her love in the end. I want you to be happy, Alex," Anne says.

Even though I'm listening to her, I'm not entirely sure that I believe her when she says that Julia will forgive me. It feels like I've done more than can be forgiven.

"I don't know, Anne."

"It's worth a try, Alex; you want this. Why not try to get it? Please, I want you to be happy. Stop punishing yourself. If she doesn't accept you after you've explained and tried, maybe it is time to let go. You can just try taking care of your children and making them know that you love them very much," Anne says, and I smile. I figure that it can't be that bad and that it is best that I try; if she says no, then I won't die.

I make up my mind to think about what my sister said and consider her suggestion. I know that it's something that will require a lot of courage from me.

After Anne leaves, I call Julia. I don't wait for her call this time.

"Hello, Julia. "How are you today?" I ask, and I can almost hear her smile at the other end of the phone.

"I'm fine. The children are still in school; you can't talk to them now."

"I'll call back later to speak with them. I just want to talk with you. It's been a while."

"Oh, okay. What are we talking about?" Julia asks, and I can hear the surprise in her voice. We've barely had any form of conversation that didn't involve the children previously.

"You never really told me where you grew up."

Julia seems excited to talk about herself, and for the rest of the day, we talk about everything and nothing, and I feel myself growing more and more in love with her. Maybe I won't make it to Australia just yet.

***

Julia

"I miss Daddy," Layla says. We're all seated in the living room. It's Saturday, and it has been two weeks since we saw Alex. He's been calling the children every other day, but he hasn't made any plans to visit yet. Today, though, he hasn't called, and we're all waiting for my phone to ring. It's almost like he is a superstar at this point.

"I miss your dad too," I say. Even after Maya talked to me, I haven't found the courage to tell Alex anything. I'm waiting until he comes to Australia at the end of the month to see the children. We've been talking a bit more, though, even if I can tell that he is skeptical. I'm trying to forgive him, and I can feel myself making progress. These days, I want to ask him why he was so sure the child wasn't his. The character he portrayed that day seems nothing like him now. I can agree that it has been a long time, and the probability that he has changed with time is very high, but then again, he wasn't such a terrible person when we had our night together. I can remember very well, he was very loving. The memory isn't one that I go back to very often; I usually avoid it, because I don't like what comes after.

"Will Daddy not come here?" Landon asks, and I sigh. I don't want to tell the children that Alex is already planning a trip because I don't know if something will stop him from making it, and they will be so devastated if he doesn't. I will be devastated too, but I don't really have anyone shielding me.

"Your daddy will call very soon," I say. Luca is about to say something when my phone rings. As though planned, it is Alex calling.

I pick up the call immediately.

"Hey, Julia. "You never did tell me where exactly you lived," he says immediately after I pick up the call. I didn't realize that I would be so excited to talk to him; my pulse rate has increased, and I'm trying to calm myself. It takes a while before I understand what he's saying.

"My address? What do you need my address for?" I ask. I'm surprised that he's asking.

"Oh, you know, maybe if I am coming to visit you or something." He sounds playful, and I start to sense that something else is going on. What is he talking about?

"Where are you, Alex?" I ask at the same time Layla drags on my shirt; she wants me to let her talk to her father. My daughter became a daddy's girl so easily.

97

"I may or may not be at the airport in Sydney," he says again, and there's still that playing tone in his voice.

"What?" I shout and stand up immediately. The children stand up with me. "Are you serious?" I ask as I pick up my car keys. I'm more excited about Alex being so close than I thought I would be.

"Yes, I am very serious," he says; this time his voice is serious.

"I am coming to the airport," I say, disconnecting the call.

"Mommy, you didn't let us talk to Daddy," Layla whines.

"Don't worry, darling; very soon, you will see him face to face," I say, and the children look at me oddly.

"Daddy is here?" Luca asks.

"Yes, love, let's go pick him up at the airport," I say, and they all follow me to the car. It's a wonder that I don't get a ticket as I drive to the airport. It's not until I have arrived and am looking for Alex that I stop to wonder why I'm so excited about this.

"Julia!" I turn when I hear my name. It's only when I see Alex that I know that I have forgiven him. All I feel is love for him; there is no undertone of hate or anger. I run to him and hug him tight. The children are running behind me, and I feel their small hands around us.

"Alex," I whisper. I know that he can see that I love him. I can see it in his eyes, too.

"I am really sorry, Julia," he says, and I nod my head. He doesn't have to say it; it doesn't matter if he says it or not. I know that he is sorry, and I have let go.

"I love you," I whisper against his lips.

God, I love you," he says, pressing his lips against mine.

"Daddy!" Layla shouts, and the kiss is over before it starts.

"Pumpkin," Alex says, and he lets me go pick up our daughter. I have never been so jealous of someone and yet so happy for them. I can see the love that he has for her, and I'm so happy for my daughter that she has a father who loves her.

"Daddy!" Luca and Landon shout together, and they all hug him.

"Come on, loves, let's go home," I say to my children and their father, and he smiles at me.

The children don't want to leave their father, and so it's hard for us to have any privacy to talk. Leo comes along a few hours after Alex is around, and I introduce the two of them. They both seem amenable to each other. Leo is the one who takes the children away for a little while.

I feel nervous when I'm alone with Alex. I want to say something, but I'm afraid to actually start.

"I'm really sorry, Julia."

"You don't have to say that all the time. You did wrong at the time, but I have forgiven you," I say, and he looks so relieved.

"I cannot believe that you actually love me after what I've done. I know that I don't have any excuse, but my last girlfriend, Genevieve, was pregnant when we broke up. I usually used a condom with her, but when she told me she was pregnant, I accepted it, and for months she fooled me. If I hadn't caught her in bed with my friend, Jack, at the time, I would have taken care of another man's child without knowing. Over time, a lot of women also came to me claiming to be pregnant with my child, and none of them ended up being my baby; they all just wanted money, and I expected you to be like them."

I feel so bad that I was compared to other women, yet I understand that I am also angry at all the women who tried to fool Alex into having their child; they are all part of this.

"I should add that I feared I would be too attached to you, which is why I didn't stay till morning that night. I have always had feelings for you, and I planned to look for you; seeing you tell me that you were pregnant made me angry. I felt like you were just like the others that wanted me for my money. I was so wrong, Julia, and I'm paying for that; I missed the first 6 years of my children's lives," he says, and I nod my head. I already forgave him, so the apology just gives me justification; he didn't do it without reason, and I still love him.

I move closer to him and wrap my arms around him.

"I love you," I say as he places his lips against mine.

"And I love you."

ONE YEAR LATER

"Mommy, Landon took my pencil!" Layla shouts, and I look and see that Landon is looking very sheepish.

"Give your sister back her pencil. If you want a pencil, you can simply ask," I say to my son.

"She says she will give me the pencil if I help with her math assignment," he says.

"But you didn't help me with the assignment; you only showed me how to do it," Layla says, and I roll my eyes at both of them.

"Landon, do you need another pencil?" I ask him, and he shakes his head.

"Then give your sister back her pencil. She's your sister; she doesn't have to pay you before you teach her something," I say, and he nods.

Luca is sitting in the living room drawing something, so at least he's not making so much noise. He is my only child who is quiet.

"You all shouldn't stress your mother so much," Alex says. I didn't even hear him when he came in. He's looking so handsome, just like the first day I met him.

"Look how strained your face looks. Smile for me, love," he says after he hugs me, and I smile.

He rubs his hand on my enlarged stomach with a smile.

"I can't wait to have our fourth child." Four is a massive number. "I never thought you would be so excited about number four," Alex says, and I laugh. We got married ten months ago, as soon as we could manage, and I moved into his apartment with the children. Ever since, we have been in love and living together. I got pregnant again not too long after we got married. Unlike my first pregnancy, which came with fear, I have been so excited about this one. I wanted the baby; we even planned for it.

"I am so lucky to have you, Julia. I'm so lucky to have all of you," Alex says, and I smile.

"So am I. I love you."

ABOUT THE AUTHOR

Natacha Jean is the author of the romance novel **The Weight of a Broken Heart**. The novel is her first published novel. She enjoys reading, cooking, and spending time with her family in her spare time. Additionally, she enjoys spending time outdoors, hiking, gardening, and traveling. She currently resides with her spouse and two children in Connecticut.

Made in the USA
Middletown, DE
16 July 2023

35301885R00060